GUARDIANS OF THE RAILWAY

To My Dear Friends,
Jennifer and David,

GUARDIANS OF THE RAILWAY

"Mark 2".

With Every good Wish.

MICHAEL VALLOW

Michael

28th May 2020

Guardians of the Railway published in Great Britain in 2020

Written by Michael Vallow

Copyright © Michael Vallow 2020

A CIP catalogue record for this book is available from the British Library.

Paperback ISBN 978-1-9162251-1-4

Book cover design by: Daisa & Co Publishing

Book typeset by:
DAISA & CO PUBLISHING
Barton upon Humber
North Lincolnshire
United Kingdom
DN18 5JR
www.daisapublishing.com

Printed in England

Daisa & Co Publishing is committed to a sustainable future for our business, our readers and our planet.
This book is made from paper certified by the Forestry Stewardship Council (FSC), an organisation dedicated to promoting responsible management of forest resources

Dedication

"If you seek his Memorial

Look around you"

George Robert Cryer MP Bsc. Econ

(Plaque at Haworth Station, Keighley and Worth
Valley Railway)

‡

I was riding on the Settle-Carlisle Railway from Leeds
more than twenty-five years ago when it stopped in
Keighley Station. I noticed and took in the olde-
worlde charm of the part of the station which is home
to the Worth Valley line and decided to ride on it as
soon as possible. I have done so at least once a year
ever since.

Campaigners like Bob Cryer ensured that the line,
which had closed six years earlier, reopened in 1968.

Such campaigns are part of the story of all heritage railways, whose continuation also owes to the volunteers who run them and the many visitors who ride on them. The experience of the bygone "age of steam" has thus been preserved for the pleasure and education of present and future generations.

The Settle-Carlisle line itself faced the threat of closure which never happened because of the strength of public opinion and it remains part of the national railway network.

I dedicate this book to such past and present campaigners and volunteers who welcome visitors young and old. I have been on many heritage railways now and they give great pleasure to many people.

For that, I thank you.

Contents

Prologue

The Most Perfect Paper Aeroplane in the World

Marcus Redlands shuffled. He was engrossed in his task. He intended, quite simply, to make the most technically brilliant paper aeroplane in the world.

He would not, of course, have been busy with his aircraft design if Mr Moss, the Geography Master (and one of the most disliked teachers in the school) had been sitting at his desk. He would instead have been doing what he was supposed to be doing – writing an essay about the people of Zambia and their daily lives.

Mr Moss was generally assumed to have eyes in the back of his head. Though he had walked out of the classroom not five minutes ago, telling the second years that he would be away for twenty minutes, not one of them had dared to look at their notes or the textbook to help them with their essay.

They had been asked to learn about the subject for their homework and this was a test. The consequences of cheating, they suspected, would be little short of being skinned alive. Of course, things might not be too pleasant if they didn't do very well in the test either...

Marcus knew that Geography wasn't his best subject at school. He had not spent the time he should have studying this last night and he would not be getting a good mark when the essay was returned to him.

He felt sure Mr Moss would have a few sharp words to say to him on the subject of doing his homework properly. The one consolation was that it was Thursday and the work would not be returned duly marked until next week. For now, the paper aeroplane was taking Marcus' mind off such worries. The twelve-year-old boy studied his handiwork. He was quite experienced at making paper aeroplanes and had torn out the middle pages of quite a few exercise books to improve his skills. Yes, there was no doubt about it, this was the best one so far.

The wooden desks were laid out in six straight rows and Marcus was sitting at the back and towards the right of the classroom. He looked across to the windows on the opposite side of the room. A small window at the top was open. It seemed a shame to sacrifice this great technical achievement but Marcus was convinced that he could throw his paper aeroplane straight out of the window. He was sure he had a good aim and wouldn't even need to stand up...

He would have to make a replacement, of course, as well as leave himself a few minutes to write something about Zambia. Two middle pages were as much as he felt he could safely tear out of his Geography exercise book without the risk of it being noticed, but he had only torn one out so far. He looked across at the window and lined up the nose of his aeroplane so that it was at just the right angle. He presumed that being a pilot was like this!

Trudi Barnes, sitting towards the front of the classroom on the left-hand side, put down her fountain pen and glanced at the sheet of paper in front of her. She had spent an hour studying this topic yesterday evening – longer than pupils were supposed to spend on their homework. She had thought that Mr Moss might ask a few questions about it at the start of the lesson but having to write an essay about it for the whole of the lesson had been something of a shock to her (and to the rest of the class). She was sure she wouldn't be getting very good marks for this...

It was Thursday 22nd September 1966. It was almost three weeks since the start of the school term. Form 2R would have to endure Mr Moss as their Geography teacher for another ten months. Would they survive?

Marcus Redlands took one final look at the window he was aiming for. Yes, there would be nothing more satisfying than seeing his creation flying cleanly through the window and straight down into the playground below. He almost felt like clapping his hands to invite the others to watch – but the classroom door was open, and he didn't want to attract the attention of any teacher who might be passing...

Trudi Barnes felt a sense of panic coming over her. She had written a little over a page and now her mind had gone blank. She could not think of anything further to write. She tried desperately to rack her brains – she had read all about this last night. She felt a sense of terror at the thought of getting into trouble with Mr Moss, but it was no good. She had put her pen down and it didn't seem as if she was about to pick it back up in a hurry.

Marcus admired his handiwork one final time. 'Here goes,' he thought, launching it into the air.

Trudi felt as if somebody was ruffling her red hair. Then a paper aeroplane landed on her desk. She froze; where had this come from?

Marcus had watched as the paper aeroplane soared into the air and cursed as it dropped down again a little short of the open window. It brushed through the hair of that red-headed girl – what was her name, Barnes? – and then landed on her desk.

What a waste. It had been a brilliant paper aeroplane and he had been convinced it would fly straight out of the window. He would make another immediately – and this one *would* fly out of the window.

Then he had second thoughts. Nobody, he guessed, had seen him launch that first paper plane. If he did it again just now, they might. It would have to wait. Disappointed, he turned to the blank piece of paper in front of him. Time to write something about Zambia, even if he didn't know a lot about it.

Then a broad grin broke out over his face.

So what if he hadn't managed to send his paper aeroplane out of the window! He had given that red-headed girl quite a fright when it landed first on her hair and then on her desk. She still looked quite startled – this was much more fun than his original plan!

The piece of paper in front of him stayed blank as Marcus continued to study Trudi Barnes. They got on the same train every morning and evening yet they had never spoken to each other outside school – or in school either, apart from a couple of occasions when teachers had put them in the same group for an exercise. Of course, they were completely different. She was a Teacher's Pet for whom life was easy – she was always getting top marks in her work. Obviously a bit of a snob, too – otherwise why hadn't she spoken to him on the train?

Marcus was not in the least distressed by the thought that the paper aeroplane might have distracted Trudi and caused her to do less well in the test. Quite the opposite – he gloated at the prospect of her being brought down to earth.

After a moment, Trudi decided that she must do something about the paper aeroplane – she didn't want to be caught by Mr Moss with it on her desk. Her first thought was to take it to the bin at the front of the classroom, next to the teacher's desk. Then she heard footsteps approaching the classroom.

'Better put it in my schoolbag,' she thought.

She was leaning down to her satchel, paper aeroplane in hand, when Mr Moss walked through the door.

"Just what is that, young lady?"

Trudi froze. She knew very well that she was being addressed. She might have been amused by the stupid question if she hadn't been so petrified.

"A paper aeroplane, sir." Trudi straightened herself up but her voice sounded faint.

"A paper aeroplane, eh? You've nothing better to do with your time when I am out of the room than make a paper aeroplane?"

"I didn't make it, sir. It just landed on my desk."

"It – just – landed – on – your desk." The Geography Master repeated the words slowly and deliberately.

Trudi realised that her story probably didn't sound very convincing. Perhaps someone else could tell Mr Moss that they saw it flying towards her desk?

"Would anyone like to admit that they just threw a paper aeroplane on to Miss Barnes' desk?" The question was asked in a sneering tone and the elderly teacher glanced round the room. Nobody spoke. Marcus, not wishing to catch the schoolmaster's eye, looked down.

"Well, we didn't get very far with that one," said Mr Moss. "Perhaps you would like to tell me, Miss Barnes, why you were putting the paper aeroplane – which – just – landed – on -your – desk into your schoolbag?"

Trudi felt her face becoming redder than ever. "I… didn't want you to see it, sir."

The Geography Master exploded, "I'll bet you didn't!" he exclaimed. He picked up the essay from Trudi's desk. "That's all you write in the test, you spend the rest of the time making a paper aeroplane and you didn't want me to see it. Should I be surprised?"

"It isn't true, sir. I didn't make it."

"Truth – you wouldn't know the meaning of the word, girl!" shouted Mr Moss. Trudi hated him more than ever for that – nobody had ever called her a liar before.

The Master added, coldly, "You're in serious trouble young lady, wasting my lesson time then lying and being cheeky. You can write me a three page essay on... *Why I mustn't make paper aeroplanes in class'*. You're fortunate that I am taking detention next week and I'm hoping that there will be nobody in it, or I wouldn't be so lenient."

With that, he turned to the rest of the class: "All right, the pantomime's over. Get on with your essays and they'd better be good."

Trudi was relieved that her ordeal was over – though there was still that wretched essay to write tonight of course; not to mention the one she was supposed to be doing now – the last five minutes had not helped to give her any ideas for that...

A few minutes later, all of the pupils were relieved that their ordeal was over when the final bell of the day rang. Marcus was half-way up the school drive when he felt a sharp kick in his shin. Expecting an apology, he turned around to see the tall blonde-haired figure of Sarah Wilson-Hampton, a girl in his form.

"It was very brave of you to admit making that plane in Geography a few minutes ago," she said with heavy sarcasm. "Anyway, Trudi might not know who was responsible, but I do. So if you haven't apologised to her by the end of school tomorrow, Big Boy, I'll tell her myself."

With that, the tall girl strolled off into the distance as Marcus called out (probably deliberately when she was out of earshot) "Why don't you mind your own business?"

"She's right, you know," said Marcus' friend Dave, who was next to him. "You shouldn't have let the girl take the rap like that."

"I'd have confessed if she'd got into serious trouble." replied Marcus uncomfortably.

"Oh yeah?" answered Dave before striding off. Marcus genuinely believed what he had just said, but it seemed that he was the only one who did.

Chapter 1

The Last Day of School

"Watch it!"

Marcus looked at Trudi Barnes' angry face and cursed. If the two members of the same form were to speak to one another at Banham Station, where each had caught the train to Royds Well in the morning for the past year or so to go to school, he wouldn't have chosen those as the first two words to be exchanged.

Now Trudi had the effrontery to be annoyed with him - for something which wasn't his fault. Some young kids from a Youth Club, who had been milling about the station until the train came in, had started pushing as the passengers boarded the train and as a result, Marcus had kicked Trudi's heel as she was climbing into the carriage.

Usually there was plenty of room on the 8:10 train, but not this morning. As Marcus headed to the middle of the carriage, he realised with horror that the kids had filled the seats in front as well as behind him.

Trudi had just sat down, and so Marcus had a choice. He sat opposite her or he stood for the half-hour journey - there were plenty of kids ready to take the seat if he didn't.

'I'm not letting that stuck-up girl think I'm frightened of her.' thought Marcus, as he plumped himself down in the seat. If Trudi considered she had a grievance against him that morning, Marcus could think of plenty of reasons why he had never liked her...

For a start, she was always so smartly turned out. Not a single hair of her long red mane was ever out of place. He glanced at the girl out of the corner of his eye – yes, today was no different. Her tie was neat and so was the rest of the uniform; her brown blazer, in better condition than his own, and a smart black skirt. Then there was the fact that she always came top of the form in almost every subject, without apparently making a lot of effort. Marcus worked hard - even if he didn't admit it – but he struggled to achieve average results.

Worst of all, there was that embarrassing incident a few weeks ago when he had made a paper aeroplane and aimed it at an open window. It had instead landed on Trudi's desk and Mr Moss, the somewhat fierce Geography Master, had returned to the classroom unexpectedly, seen it there and ticked her off about it.

He hadn't been unduly concerned about the matter until an interfering girl from his form, Sarah Wilson Hampton, had blackmailed him (as he saw it) into making an apology. His best friend Dave had been a bit funny about it too. Anyway, he had approached Trudi the following morning and tried both to apologise and make light of the matter. This had been spectacularly badly received, with the crushing words, "Marcus, I would accept your apology if I thought you were making one."

"Just apologise, Marcus." The interfering Sarah Wilson Hampton, who had taken a continuing interest in the matter, had thrown in. He had, and it had been accepted, but having been forced to do so rankled…

'One thing about it,' thought Marcus. 'I won't need to worry about making conversation with her. I expect she'll stick her nose into a French book and prepare three lessons ahead.'

Despite telling himself that he was not remotely curious about Trudi, Marcus found himself wondering what life was like in the Barnes household. She would doubtless be the perfect daughter, for Marcus was sure that she could say 'Yes', 'No' and 'Three Bags Full' right on cue. He looked at her again, discreetly, hoping she wouldn't notice. She was small and slender. Though it hadn't been gentle this morning, her voice was generally soft, and to Marcus' ears, a little posh.

Marcus wanted the girl to be human, so he could forgive her all of this. If she could get red marks on her work like the rest of the class, if she could get her French verbs wrong occasionally - above all, if she could misbehave and get told off once in a while. (The incident with Mr Moss a few weeks ago didn't count, as it wasn't her fault). Marcus doubted that Trudi had ever done anything wrong in her life. If she had, it would make her far more endearing.

Trudi noticed with disdain that the boy was looking at her, for all his efforts to pretend otherwise. She had not taken much interest in Marcus. He was intelligent, but too often ready to play the fool to get on with the other boys; and he was so scruffy – he seemed not to care about his appearance, even at the start of the day.

Then there was the incident with the paper aeroplane. He had made it and thrown it but hadn't had the courage to admit this to Mr Moss when he saw it on Trudi's desk. So he had allowed her to take the blame for it. He had apologised the following day, she suspected because he had been seen by classmates who had told him to do so. Even then, the apology had seemed half-hearted to her.

She could have very little respect for somebody who would let an innocent party be blamed for their own wrongdoing, rather than confess to it, so they were unlikely to be great friends anytime soon…

Trudi glanced out of the window.

"I say!" she suddenly exclaimed, quite forgetting she was speaking to someone who had kicked her heel not two minutes before. "Have you seen that notice?"

Marcus looked out of the window and spotted the notice, attached to a station lamppost, which must have startled Trudi. It was headed in large letters:

NOTICE OF CLOSURE OF RAILWAY LINE BANHAM TO ROYDS WELL

Just then, the train set off with a jerk, so Marcus was unable to read the smaller print underneath. He was, however, able to read the last line:-

Closure of the railway line will take place on Friday 31st March 1967.

Most pupils at Royds Well High School either walked to school or travelled by bus or in their parents' cars. His classmates were envious of Marcus for being able to travel on the old steam train.

It seemed as if they wouldn't have reason to be envious any longer - this was a bitter blow.

"What can we do?" asked Trudi, clearly as upset as he was about this.

"I don't suppose there's much we can do," replied Marcus. It seemed unlikely now that Trudi would be sticking her nose in a French book on this journey.

"We can't let them just close the railway like that." she said.

"How do we stop them? It's their railway - we can't exactly buy it from them." answered Marcus.

There was silence. Trudi knew this as well as Marcus, but she didn't like him saying it. They were so powerless - Trudi and Marcus Against the World (this was a somewhat unexpected alliance). What could they do?

Marcus broke the silence: "Are you doing anything over half term?"

Trudi perked up. "I'd forgotten it was the last day of school today. We're not going anywhere, but it will be nice to be on holiday. I can stay in bed a bit longer in the morning."

"I'm not going away either, but I never get bored when I'm not at school."

"Or when you're in school either!" Trudi laughed, thinking of the times Marcus had played about in class and annoyed his teachers.

"All right, so some of us are better at schoolwork than others."

"Some of us concentrate in lessons and some of us don't."

Both were smiling as they spoke these words. Trudi no longer felt that she was sitting opposite a buffoon. Marcus no longer felt that he was sitting opposite a

Miss Goody-Two-Shoes. For the rest of the journey, they chatted like old friends about school, teachers and classmates.

It was incredible to think that less than half an hour ago they had almost been strangers. Marcus grinned as the train pulled into Royds Well station and the two pupils stood up, ready to get off.

"We'd better not speak to one another once we're outside the station!"

"Why not? It's not against the law!"

"It might not be, but it won't do my image much good if I'm seen talking to you."

Trudi punched Marcus playfully, "I hope there's a bit more room on the train this evening."

"Why?"

"So I don't have to sit next to you!"

The two twelve-year-olds walked along the road away from the station, deep in thought. They turned into the street where the school was situated and walked down the drive into Royds Well High School.

They entered the Form Room one after the other, splitting up to go to their separate desks. Neither mentioned the railway as they chatted to their friends, though it was on both their minds.

Miss Loxley, their form mistress, arrived later than usual that morning, at about 8:55 and hastily took the register before the pupils made their way to the assembly hall. It was a Friday morning, the day on which pupils could expect to listen to a lecture from the Headmistress on the misdeeds of some of their number. Today was no exception.

"I'd just like to say a few words before you all go to your classes." said Mrs Hampshire at the end of the assembly. She always began like that.

'That means we'll be here for another ten minutes,' thought Marcus. 'Still,' he consoled himself, 'that's ten minutes less of our Maths lesson.'

"It has come to my attention," said the Headmistress, "that some of you have been getting sloppy about your school uniform. Very sloppy. Now the reason we wear uniform..."

"Where do you live?" Trudi, who was sitting next to him, was whispering in his ear in assembly. Marcus nearly fell off his chair. He might have been daring before now, but he had never been quite as daring as that.

He glanced along the row at Miss Loxley, who was sitting at the side of the hall. Her eyes were firmly fixed on the Headmistress at the front. With one eye on Mrs Hampshire himself, Marcus told her in a whisper.

"That's only about five minutes away from where I live. Can I call on you this evening?"

"I - suppose so." Marcus wondered what his Mother would think. She would probably approve of this gentle, polite and well-spoken girl - it would make a change from the rather rowdy boys who usually visited him.

She might even think he should spend time with Trudi rather than with them, which would never do!

"Well, you might sound more enthusiastic about it. I've got some ideas about what we might do."

"Do? You mean go for bike rides, that sort of thing?"

"No, idiot! I mean what we can do about the railway to stop them closing it."

"Oh, I see." Marcus glanced along the row of pupils to the side of the hall, this time catching Miss Loxley's eye. He glanced down, slightly shame-facedly.

"You are interested?"

Marcus nodded, fairly certain that Miss Loxley had noticed they were talking.

"… Now I want you to go away and think about what I've just said, and when you come back to school, I expect you to tighten your belts. I don't want to have to mention these things again."

There was a pause, during which there was silence in the hall. "One last thing," said Mrs Hampshire. "I hope that you all have a nice holiday and that you come back refreshed and ready to work hard for the rest of the term."

That was something else which the Headmistress said before every holiday and Marcus wished that she wouldn't. The thought of being expected to return to school refreshed and ready to work hard (almost) put him off the idea of a holiday!

After another slight pause, Mrs Hampshire added: "Thank you, you may go."

A thousand pupils began to leave the hall in an orderly manner, not pushing as they might have done at a bus stop, and very conscious of the beady eye which was watching over them.

"Right," said the normally good-humoured Miss Loxley when they were back in the classroom. "Get off to your lessons please, 2R. Marcus and Trudi, I want to speak to you before you go."

"Ooh," exclaimed other members of the class.

"Don't make silly noises, please." said Miss Loxley, irritated.

When the other pupils had filed out, Miss Loxley closed the door.

"What was Mrs Hampshire speaking about this morning, Marcus?" she asked.

"People getting sloppy about their school uniform, Miss." he replied, unconsciously straightening his tie.

"And...?"

He glanced up at her. Miss Loxley was a young teacher, perhaps three or four years out of college. Her ginger hair was tied in a ponytail, and she wore spectacles. Normally a very kindly and gentle woman, but she did not look like that just now.

"*And* she suggested we should tighten our belts, Miss."

Marcus' attempt at humour failed disastrously.

"Did you hear any more of what she said, Trudi?"

"No, Miss." She blushed, ashamed.

"I'm not surprised that neither of you heard what she said - you were both chattering away in assembly. For your information, she was talking about pupils dawdling in corridors and being late for lessons, just as you're going to be. You were very fortunate the Headmistress didn't see you - she would probably have made you stand up in front of the whole school."

Trudi looked horrified and Marcus felt uncomfortable.

"By rights, I should put the pair of you in detention." The teacher continued a little more softly. "It is almost the half term holiday and I suppose, I might have forgotten about it by the time we come back. I'm particularly surprised at you, Trudi, you're normally very well-behaved."

The girl looked embarrassed.

"Right, you two," said Miss Loxley, a little more sharply. "Get to your lessons now - and try to stay out of trouble for the rest of the day!"

Chapter 2

Half Term Holidays - At Last!

Marcus could not help but see the funny side of it. Just over an hour ago, he had been thinking that Trudi would seem a little more human if she could receive an occasional telling-off and now she *had* been told off!

If Trudi was gaining brownie-points with Marcus however, she certainly wasn't with the teachers. "Stay out of trouble," Miss Loxley had said. That was proving easier said than done.

Only one thing seemed to occupy Trudi's mind that morning – what she and Marcus could do to save the railway. This was unfortunate, because her teachers seemed to have other things on their minds, such as the subjects they were trying to teach. She was mildly rebuked in French and English for not concentrating in class; in Geography, one of her few weaker subjects, she was given one hundred lines for not being able to point out Zambia on the map, after her class had spent a considerable period studying that country.

Word had just got back to Miss Loxley, who spoke to the girl once more at lunchtime.

"Trudi, is something wrong?"

"No, Miss." The girl did not imagine that her teacher would be interested in a campaign to save a railway line - after all, most of the staff seemed to have their own cars.

Miss Loxley frowned. "Well, I must say I've been hearing a lot of complaints about you this morning. According to the other teachers, you don't seem to have been with it at all. Just pull your socks up next half term, will you?"

Marcus, who had overheard this conversation, was busy putting some books away in his desk. Turning away from the teacher now that the interview was over, Trudi glanced at him.

Marcus made an exaggerated gesture of kneeling down and pulling his socks up. His new partner-in-crime wanted to laugh but did not dare.

"I could have killed you," she told him a few minutes later when she joined him in the playground. "Pulling your socks up like that - I did so want to giggle!"

"Well," laughed Marcus. "I thought I would pull my socks up before the holiday rather than after!"

"You are a comic." Trudi was thinking that Marcus was one of the most amusing people she had ever met - all the girls in the class were much more serious.

"So I'm told," he grinned. "But listen, Trudi, we're going to have to decide which one of us is Marcus, here."

"What do you mean?"

"Well, I'm supposed to be the one who plays the fool and gets into trouble. I've been a bit worried that I've got a rival this morning. You've been told off four times and got a hundred lines and we've only had four lessons since assembly. Are you hoping to get a detention before the end of the day?"

Ouch. Suddenly her companion didn't seem quite so amusing.

"I'll do something about the railway on my own if you're not interested." said Trudi.

"I didn't say that," retorted Marcus. "I'm just saying that you're going to have to forget about the railway until the end of the day and concentrate on your lessons. Not much point in getting into trouble, is there?"

"I'm sorry Marcus, you're right. Perhaps I'd better pull my socks up before the holiday, like you!"

Trudi suddenly put her arm round a rather startled Marcus. "We're going to make a great team, aren't we?"

"We'll do our best," he replied.

The girl looked serious, "What can we do, Marcus? It seemed so simple this morning when I was thinking about it in assembly - get everybody to protest about it to the railway company and then they would change their mind. Now I'm not so sure."

"We've got to do something like that," replied Marcus thoughtfully. "One thing's for sure - we can't buy the railway line - not unless your father can afford it anyway."

Trudi laughed. "If he can, he could give me a rise in my pocket money first. No Marcus, we have to find a way to protect it somehow."

"Hey, Marcus," shouted one of the crowd Trudi so disapproved of (or at least, so he assumed). "Are you going to play football, or are you going to spend the whole lunchtime chatting?"

Marcus turned to Trudi. "I'd better go," he said. He hesitated for a moment, grinned then added, "I was thinking this morning that you would seem a little more human if you occasionally got into trouble. I think you've already proved the point but remember, there's no need to be too human!"

With that, he dodged a friendly punch and scuttled off to join the game of football. Trudi stayed where she was for a while, watching.

Marcus was totally engrossed in the game of football now. It was strange, she thought. If there had been any other spare seats on the train that morning, she and Marcus would not have talked to one another. Yet they had now known one another for about four hours and here he was advising her to stay out of trouble - for all the times he had been in bother! The strangest part of it was, she didn't resent his advice. Trudi stood up from the wall she had been sitting on and moved away. It had been a funny old day...

That afternoon Miss Loxley called her back as the others were leaving to go to their first lesson after registration.

"Trudi?"

"Yes, Miss?" It had been a bad day, but surely Trudi couldn't have done anything wrong over the lunch break; or was sitting on a wall against school rules now?

"You're quite sure there's nothing wrong? No problems at home or anything?"

"No, Miss."

"You would tell me if there were, wouldn't you? You know that you can always talk to me."

Miss Loxley seemed anxious. Perhaps she was feeling guilty that she had spoken a little sharply to the girl that morning.

"Thank you, Miss."

"All right, Trudi. You may go."

"Who's been a naughty girl again, then?" asked Marcus light-heartedly, as she caught up with the rest of her form, waiting to go into another classroom.

"Not me." smiled Trudi, giving no further explanation.

Fortunately she was able to concentrate during her lessons that afternoon and got into no further trouble.

The final lesson of the day was History, with 2R's form teacher, Miss Loxley. Although a kindly woman, Miss Loxley was very concerned that her pupils should show good manners.

Those who had assumed that the sound of the buzzer at the end of her lessons meant they were entitled to pack their bags ready to go home had discovered to their cost that they were wrong. For their form teacher had made them empty their bags of all their books, not just those for her lesson and wait until she was ready to finish the lesson.

Today was no exception. "Right, 2R," said the teacher at the start of the lesson. "I want to make one thing clear. The half-term holiday starts at 4 o'clock, that's in forty minutes, *not now*! Okay?"

So 2R, which was fond of its form teacher, had done its best to think about the French Revolution for the last part of the day, although by the end of the lesson, its mind was definitely on the half-term holiday.

When the buzzer sounded, instinct triumphed over experience and the pupils' books were in their bags before Miss Loxley had finished speaking.

"I'm very tempted to ask the Headmistress if I can teach a different Form after the holiday," said the teacher with mock severity. "By rights, I ought to make you all turn out your bags again, but I suppose it *is* half term…"

"Thank you, Miss." chorused the class.

"All right be off with you, 2R." said Miss Loxley with a smile. "Just see that you don't annoy me when you come back!"

"Race you to the station," said Marcus to Trudi when they were outside in the corridor.

"You can *walk* in the school buildings." said Miss Loxley, who had overheard. So they did - but they ran as soon as they were outside. Trudi's friends had never seen anything like it.

The train, which was due to leave Royds Well Station at twenty-past four, was already standing in the station when Marcus and Trudi arrived there with more than ten minutes to spare. Usually, they would have climbed into the carriage and waited for their journey home to begin, but not today. Without saying a word to the other, each wanted to admire the lovely red steam engine they had seen so many times before, and the handsome brown carriages.

Both had the same thought in their minds. How could anybody be so heartless as to want to close down this wonderful branch line?

A few more people were arriving at the station now, and the two companions noticed the kids from the youth club who had been on the train that morning, in the distance. If they wanted a seat, it was time to board the train.

"You're not sitting opposite me." grinned Marcus as he almost ran down the carriage.

"Try and stop me!" laughed Trudi.

They chatted animatedly on the way home, mainly about school. They didn't talk much about how they could save the railway - there would be time enough to discuss that during the holiday.

When they got to the station at Banham, the two companions studied the notice about the railway line closure: -

---

NOTICE OF CLOSURE OF RAILWAY LINE BANHAM TO ROYDS WELL

Notice is hereby given according to statute of the intention of the railway company to close the Branch Line from Banham to Royds Well. Objections to the proposal should be made to the Company at its Head Office. In the absence of any successful objection closure will take place on Friday 31st March 1967.

Marcus and Trudi had first seen the notice this morning, but even now it was something of a shock to read it. If they had ever given it thought, they would have expected to ride on the steam train for as long as they were at school, but, according to this notice, the line would be closed in a little over five months' time.

As they handed in their tickets, the two companions prepared to go their separate ways home.

"Shall I call on you this evening, about seven?" asked Trudi.

"I suppose so." Marcus was still worried that his Mother might make unfavourable comparisons between this charming young girl (as she would be sure to describe Trudi) and his other friends.

"Don't sound so enthusiastic about it," she snapped. "You can call on me, if you want."

"All right, I'll do that. About seven?"

So it was agreed. Marcus remained curious about Trudi's family. He was returning to his image of her as a "Goody-two-shoes" - even if today, she had been a Goody-two-shoes having an 'off-day'.

If Trudi's parents were as Marcus imagined them to be, he would certainly have to mind his Ps and Qs that evening. Trudi, on the other hand, was thinking about the railway. She was quite sure that she and Marcus were going to save it - but as yet, she didn't quite know how...

Chapter 3

An Unfortunate Misunderstanding

"You haven't forgotten that Fiona Loveridge is coming for tea, have you, dear?" asked Gran as Trudi walked through the door. Trudi had, of course completely forgotten about Fiona.

The two girls had been best friends from the day they first started school seven years ago. Eighteen months ago Fiona's family had moved away from the area, so now they saw one another only during the school holidays. Trudi had arranged to meet her friend at the station at ten-to-six.

"I'm sorry, I'd completely forgotten, Gran. I don't suppose we could rearrange it for tomorrow instead?"

"Of course we can't, dear," said Gran, shocked. "You really are ungracious Trudi. I've done a lot of baking today. I thought she was your best friend."

"She is, Gran." replied Trudi, realising that she had spoken foolishly.

Fiona would in any case be on her way to Royds Well Station now, if she was not already there waiting for the train to Banham.

"I'm sorry," she added, putting her arm around her grandmother.

"So am I, dear." said Gran, still feeling vexed.

Trudi turned her attention to the freshly-made buns, which smelt gorgeous. "Can I have one of those, Gran?" she asked.

"No, you can't, dear." replied Gran with a twinkle in her eye. "I've counted them all, so woe betide you if there's one missing before Fiona arrives."

Trudi smiled. Peace was restored and she knew that her grandmother had forgiven her.

There was still the awkward question of what to do about Marcus. He had told her where he lived but she couldn't remember the house number. She could hardly knock on all the doors in the street asking if Marcus lived there... Then she had a brainwave.

She checked in the telephone directory, but no, she couldn't find his address there. Perhaps his family didn't have a telephone.

She wondered briefly whether she could invite Marcus in, to join her and Fiona, when he called. Perhaps not - they might not like one another. They were certainly very different.

So there was nothing for it. She would have to wait until Marcus knocked on the door and then tell him to call another time. She wasn't looking forward to it...

She went to her bedroom to change out of her school uniform. She was feeling depressed as she put on her best dress, as she always did when Fiona was visiting. Trudi enjoyed her friend's visits and, while she was there, had never wanted to be in the company of anyone else. Tonight, she feared, would be different – her mind would be on Marcus rather than her old schoolfriend.

Walking to the station a few minutes later, Trudi desperately wished that Marcus might appear, so that she could warn him not to call. It was a forlorn hope.

All doubts were cast aside when Fiona stepped off the train however, and the two girls greeted one another as warmly as ever.

"Fee!"

"Trudi!"

The two girls gave one another a hug. It was hard to believe that it was only six weeks since they had last seen each another. Tea was a very good-humoured affair and Gran joined in the fun as much as the others. She had met Fiona on many occasions. After they had helped Gran with the washing up, the two girls went into the lounge to play some games.

Trudi had got a new game called 'Hoppit', which proved to be particularly hilarious. Gran did not disturb the girls, but Mr Barnes walked into the lounge when he got home a few minutes later.

"Whatever is that you're playing?" he asked with a grin. "I heard so much screaming and screeching I thought one of you must be ill!"

Trudi laughed. "Hoppit!" she said.

Her Father made as if to leave the room, then turned around to the girls again. "What did you say it was called?"

"Hoppit!" chorused the girls.

"Oh, I'm glad about that," he said. "I thought for a moment you were telling me to go away."

With that, he left the room, making amusing, frog-like movements as he did so.

"I like your Dad." said Fiona, a moment or so later when was out of earshot.

"So do I, Fee," replied Trudi. "Most of the time, anyway!"

A few minutes later Mr Barnes reappeared to tell Trudi he was taking Gran home. "I won't be long," he said. Trudi and her friend went to say goodbye to Gran before returning to the delights of 'Hoppit.'

Shortly after the others had gone, there was a knock on the door. Trudi glanced at the clock - it was seven o'clock. She had been enjoying herself so much she had completely forgotten about Marcus. That was the second time she had done that today. Closing the living room door as she went into the hall, Trudi opened the front door and was horrified to note that it was now raining quite hard outside. Marcus was very wet.

"I'm terribly sorry," she said. "I've got a friend with me at the moment. We'll have to talk about the railway some other time - perhaps tomorrow. Is that alright?"

A glance at his face told her that it wasn't.

"Funny how you didn't remember that a couple of hours ago." Marcus was relieved that he managed to be so restrained. After all, Trudi's parents might overhear the conversation.

"I really am sorry," she repeated. "Could you call again tomorrow, about three o'clock in the afternoon?"

"So that you can play games with me again?" he replied. "No thanks! Anyway, I'm not wasting any more time here getting wet. Goodnight!"

"Marcus…" Trudi shouted after the retreating figure, but it was too late. He was gone.

With him, she suspected, had gone her dream of them working together to save the railway. Perhaps that had always been unrealistic. After all, they were only twelve years old…

"Everything alright?" called Fiona from the lounge.

"Yes, thanks, Fee." she replied, though nothing could have been further from the truth. Tears were now welling up in her eyes. "I'm just going to the bathroom." she added.

Looking at herself in the mirror, Trudi tried to wipe away the tears. She sobbed momentarily, then told herself she must pull herself together.

Returning to the lounge five minutes later, she said, trying to sound cheerful, "Just a boy from my school calling about some homework." She was aware that she was stretching the word 'homework' a long way…

"Are you alright, Trudi?" asked her concerned friend.

"Fine, thanks, it's just that… we had… words."

Trudi finally decided that she would have to tell the truth about that. She didn't know how much of the conversation her friend had heard.

"You could have invited him in if you had wanted Trudi, I wouldn't have minded."

"It's alright, Fee. He's a hateful boy anyway." Trudi knew as she uttered these words that they were unfair and untrue.

Marcus, meanwhile, was feeling bewildered and angry as he trudged home in the wet. Only that morning he had thought of Trudi Barnes as a stuck-up girl when he had been forced to sit opposite her on the train. Then she had chatted on the journey, chatted in assembly - nearly got them both into serious trouble for that - spent part of lunchtime with him and raced him back to the station. Not to mention inviting him to her house that evening.

Now she had cried off, probably because she was worried about what her parents would think of him. Marcus had been right the first time. She was a stuck-up girl. One thing he was sure of, he wouldn't be bothering to speak to her again...

He ought to find that thought reassuring, but somehow, he didn't. After all, she had been so friendly that day, why should she be so frosty that evening? No, he told himself again, it was silly to think of her having been friendly that day. He had been right the first time. It was just a pity he had been forced to sit opposite her that morning. He should put Trudi Barnes right out of his mind.

Which, of course, he couldn't.

It took Trudi a long time to get the image of Marcus out of her mind too. She heard his words over and over again. "Funny how you didn't remember that a couple of hours ago," and "So that you can play games with me again?"

He had clearly not believed her excuse and who could blame him? It was Trudi who had forgotten that her friend was visiting, and should she not at least have invited him to shelter from the rain for a few minutes? The rain had passed over now, and Fiona had said that she wouldn't have objected.

What must Marcus have thought? With horror, Trudi wondered if he thought she was ashamed to know him – too frightened to let her Father, or her friends, meet him.

There was only one thing for it - she would have to go to the road where Marcus lived and knock on doors until she found him. She would do it the following afternoon after Fee had left. She had no choice; Marcus would not return to her house and her apology could not wait more than a week until they were back at school again. Marcus would, she was sure, forgive her. After all, they had become such great friends in the space of a single day - until he had knocked on her door that evening. So that was decided upon.

Finally Trudi was able to give her full attention to Fiona once again and the two girls enjoyed themselves as they always did. Later, they would go to bed. Fiona always slept in the bed in the spare room, while Trudi kipped down in a sleeping bag on the floor there. They would talk long after they had turned the bedroom light out and if Trudi's Father heard them, he would not say anything. At last, when they had talked about teachers, family, friends and anybody and anything else they could think of, they settled down to sleep.

Trudi dreamed about the railway. She and Marcus were in a meeting with the man in charge of it and they had just about persuaded him not to close the line from Banham to Royds Well when Marcus stood up and shouted, "No! I'm not going to have anything more to do with you, Trudi. You once sent me away from your door in the middle of driving rain!"

Trudi woke up with a sweat. She put on her torch and glanced at her watch. Half-past three in the morning. It was quite some time before she drifted off to sleep again.

The following morning the two girls went for a walk in the countryside around Banham before returning home to play some more games. After lunch, Trudi walked with her friend to the station. They gave one another a hug before Fiona climbed onto the train. They had had a very good time together. How could Trudi even have considered putting her friend off?

The two friends made promises to see one another again soon and Trudi returned home, changed her clothes and sat for about five minutes, staring into space. She was not looking forward to her next task, but it had to be done…

Chapter 4

An Apology (or two)

Trudi soon found the street where Marcus lived and knocked on the door of the first house. A kind-faced middle-aged woman answered.

"Excuse me," said the girl. "I'm looking for Marcus Redlands' house. Can you tell me where he lives?"

"He lives here. Who are you?"

"Trudi Barnes from his class at school."

The lady gave a sharp intake of breath. "So you're Trudi Barnes! He's not very pleased with you. Says you asked him to call last night and then sent him away in the pouring rain."

"Yes, I'm really sorry about that, a bit of a misunderstanding."

"You need to apologise to Marcus, not to me." said the woman a little more gently.

"That's what I'm here to do, Mrs Redlands."

"Then you'll find him in the garden shed, playing with his model railway set."

"Thank you."

"Trudi." The woman called her back. "You'll probably find he's rather cross with you, but you might be able to talk him round. Good luck."

"Thank you, Mrs Redlands."

Trudi liked Marcus' Mother and hoped that she might see more of her - if she could patch things up with Marcus.

She soon found the shed in the back garden and stood in front of the door for a moment. She was tempted to go home, but she knew that would solve nothing. She knocked on the door, with trepidation.

Marcus looked up from the model railway set, mildly annoyed by the interruption. The Blue Pullman was just about to pull out of the station.

"Come in," he called.

He was surprised at the sight which greeted him when the door opened. A girl wearing jeans and a baggy black sweater with a very familiar face - Trudi Barnes. As she walked in, she seemed much more human than the girl he had seen many times at the station and in the classroom over the past year. Perhaps they could be friends...

Then he remembered how he had been humiliated the previous evening, and anger took over.

"Go away." he said.

"I just called to say..."

"Go. Away." he repeated.

"… that I'm sorry about last night," she continued. "You see…"

"I don't need any explanations from you," he interrupted. "I know exactly what happened. You invited me to your house, and then decided that your parents wouldn't like me – that I wasn't good enough for them. So you sent me away again. That's exactly what I'm going to do to you now – don't you understand simple English? GO AWAY!"

Trudi knelt down, her knees touching the wooden floor of the shed. "I called round to say sorry and to tell you what happened." Tears were welling up in her eyes.

"Alright," he said a little more gently. He had suddenly remembered the incident of the paper aeroplane, when he had only apologised to Trudi because another pupil had forced him to do so. "Tell me what happened, but then you had better go."

"When I asked you to call round last night, I had completely forgotten that my friend Fiona Loveridge was coming to stay. We usually see one another at the holiday and Gran reminded me about it when I got home. I would have warned you but I couldn't remember which house you said you lived at. So when you arrived at the door, I couldn't think of anything to do except to send you home again. Of course, I should have invited you in, especially since it was raining so hard, but I wasn't sure whether Fee would like you - not everybody does." she added nervously, not quite realising what she had just said.

Suddenly, Marcus burst out laughing. "I could give you a list as long as your arm of people who don't like me!" he said.

"I hope you don't think I'm on that list!" said Trudi, relieved that the tension seemed to have eased between them.

Marcus looked more earnest and said: "You would be happy to let me meet your parents, wouldn't you? I mean, you're not ashamed of knowing me?"

"I'd be very happy for you to meet my Father."

"And your Mother?"

"Mum's dead. She died when I was eight."

"I'm sorry, Trudi."

"So am I. Her death was a great shock to me and Dad and we miss her terribly - but that was four years ago and we've got used to living on our own now."

"I'm sorry," Marcus repeated. "Listen Trudi, I've said some stupid things to you this afternoon. Can you forgive me?"

"Of course I can, Marcus," she smiled. "Can you forgive me for the fact you got wet-through last night?"

"Of course I can, Trudi. Like you said, it was a simple mistake. In any case, I called you all sorts of rude names in my mind afterwards,"

"Such as?"

Marcus blushed, "You wouldn't like to know. Anyway, you don't need to kneel at my feet for the rest of the afternoon. Stand up, Trudi!"

Trudi laughed: "Was that an order?"

Marcus grinned. "I couldn't order you about even if I wanted to."

"I notice you didn't turn the train set off when I arrived."

Marcus blushed again, then laughed: "If you remember, I wasn't expecting you to stay very long," he replied, "but I hope that you'll stay now. I'll get you a seat and we can watch the model trains for a few minutes - if you want, that is."

"Of course I want."

Trudi had never been very interested in model railway sets before. To her, they had just seemed like little trains going around endlessly on a little circuit, as she had told her Father very firmly when he had offered her a set the previous Christmas. Her Father had seemed rather put out, and afterwards she had suspected that he wanted the set for himself but didn't dare buy it in case she thought he was being childish.

She would tell him about Marcus' model railway when she got home.

This set consisted of a little train – or rather, two trains - going around endlessly on a little circuit, but there was so much more to it than that. The stations, the little signs which lit up, the houses, cars and even little people which made up a village, the fields and the hill which ran to the back of the board, covering part of the track and leaving only a tunnel for the trains to go in and out.

"How did you make that, Marcus?" asked Trudi, nodding towards the hill.

"Papier Mache," he replied.

"At least nobody's going to shut that line down, anyway." said Trudi a little sadly, remembering the steam train which ran from Banham to Royds Well.

Marcus grinned. "Nobody except my Mother, anyway. She says the set uses a lot of electricity and gives her big bills. She comes to watch it sometimes though."

"What about your Father? Does he like it?"

"He died too, when I was about five."

"I'm sorry."

There was silence for a few minutes as the two watched the trains go around the track.

It was no wonder Marcus' Mother complained about the electricity - there were lights on the stations, a light at the front of one of the trains and even some of the carriages were lit up. As the afternoon got darker, the train board, which took up most of the space in the shed, looked more and more attractive.

"Do you think we can do anything about the railway? From Banham, I mean?" Trudi broke the silence.

"It would be a shame if we didn't at least try."

"So what should we do?"

"Try to persuade local people to protest about it, I suppose, like you suggested. There must be a lot of people here in the village who don't want them to close the line down."

"I don't know," replied Trudi uncertainly. "There aren't many passengers when we go to school, are there?"

"Only when I kick your heels," said Marcus with a grin.

Trudi blushed, "Did I give you a bit of a telling off?"

"You said, 'watch it' and looked as if you could have killed me."

"I didn't know you then."

"Don't worry, you would probably still do the same again!"

"We were talking about the railway…"

"So we were. I suppose that we could organise a petition, perhaps even a demonstration, but we would have to hope that people would turn up for that."

"I don't think I'd better invite my Father if we do that. I'm not sure he would approve at all."

"Nor my Mother." Marcus smiled. "It seems our parents have a lot in common."

"What about chatting with the Station Master," suggested Trudi. "He seems like a nice man. He might tell us why the railway company wants to close the line."

"Good idea, Trudi. Why don't we go down at the usual time on Monday morning and speak to him then? He's always around when the train is about to leave."

Trudi grinned. "I like to have a lie-in when it's the school holidays," she said. "but I suppose we can."

"We should also do some posters," said Marcus, "and see if the local shops will put them in the windows."

"We could advertise the demonstration on them." said Trudi eagerly.

"Yes, we could. I feel as if this campaign is really coming on now and we've hardly started."

"So when do we do the posters?"

Marcus glanced at his watch. "Nearly teatime, that's a shame. Why don't we do them afterwards?"

"My house, seven o'clock?"

"Alright, but this time, if you try to keep me out, I'll knock your front door down!"

They both laughed.

"I presume we're friends now?" Trudi asked shyly, remembering the previous evening and the trouble it had caused between them.

"Of course we are." Marcus slapped his hand on to her shoulder.

"I do wish I'd let you in last night, you know."

"Life would have been much duller if you had. I wouldn't have got wet-through, and we would have had nothing to have a blazing row about!"

"Exactly."

"See you, Trudi."

The girl glanced at her watch. "I need to go for tea too, or I'll be late."

Marcus watched with amusement as Trudi raced towards the front gate. He was glad she had been to see him and remembered with a shudder how he had nearly refused to listen to her. Knowing Trudi Barnes was going to be fun.

"Dad?" said Trudi when they had finished tea.

"Yes?"

"Do you have any large pieces of paper, poster size?"

"What do you want them for?"

"What Daddy doesn't know…"

"I sometimes worry about you, Trudi. You work hard during the term, if your reports are to be believed, but as to what you get up to in your spare time…"

"As I said, what Daddy doesn't know." She grinned.

He rolled his eyes, smiled and said, "Yes, I have some large paper, and I suppose I won't ask what you want to do with it…"

By the time Marcus arrived, Trudi had already drawn a beautiful picture of a steam railway engine. The boy admired it and told her she could do the artwork.

"You can do the rest of the posters as well if you like," he said. When Marcus left at half-past nine, they had made eight posters with the caption:

SAVE OUR RAILWAY
DON'T LET THEM CLOSE IT

In smaller writing at the bottom of the poster Marcus had written:

DEMONSTRATION OUTSIDE THE TOWN HALL
WEDNESDAY 2ND NOVEMBER.

The posters, made by using different coloured felt-tip pens, were bright and eye-catching and the two schoolfriends were proud of them. Trudi felt pleased with herself when she went to bed that night. She had already saved her friendship with Marcus that day. Now there was just the small matter of the railway...

Chapter 5

A Chat with the Station Master

"I thought you youngsters were on holiday. Have you come to catch the train or bother me?"

The Station Master had a twinkle in his eye as he asked this question.

Marcus laughed. "To bother you." he replied.

"Then it's a pity you young'uns get such long holidays," said the Station Master. "School was a lot harder in my day, I can tell you - but I've got a train to wave off, so if you want to speak to me you'll have to wait patiently for ten minutes." Marcus and Trudi sat down on the rather uncomfortable wooden seat on the platform.

"I've heard enough about the bad old days from Dad." Trudi said, grinning.

Marcus nodded and laughed. "The Station Master is older than your Father - he must be nearly sixty-five. I expect schooldays were even worse in those days!"

He paused before adding, "I like your Dad."

"So do I," replied Trudi, "when he's not talking about the bad old days."

After a moment's silence, she continued: "I like your Mum, too - even though she was telling me off for being so beastly to you!"

"Telling you off?"

"Not really, I suppose. Just warning me that you were furious with me, which was quite true."

"With good reason," Marcus replied, smiling. "Mum likes you too, actually. Said you were very polite. Got me into trouble, really."

"Trouble?"

"Well, Mum always says that my friends never really talk to her, they just grunt. She reckons I ought to spend more time with you. I've no intention of doing so, of course." He dodged a friendly punch. "So we'll just save the railway and then I'll never speak to you again." Marcus continued outrageously.

Trudi stuck her tongue out at him - at the very moment the Station Master turned to speak to them.

The girl blushed. "I'm very sorry," she said. "That was meant for Marcus, not for you."

"If I was a teacher, you'd have been for it in my day," said the Station Master, good-humouredly. "and quite rightly too. You youngsters have no discipline today."

Trudi's face was now the colour of beetroot and Marcus was trying desperately not to laugh.

"You two go into my office," said the older man. "I think I can trust you not to pinch anything. I'll only be another five minutes or so."

Once in the office, Marcus could contain himself no longer. He burst out laughing.

"Oh, Trudi," he said after a couple of minutes. "That was so funny. You looked like a naughty schoolgirl who had just been caught misbehaving."

"I felt like one," she replied sheepishly. "Fancy my sticking my tongue out just then – I hope he didn't think I was sticking it out at him."

"Of course he didn't," said Marcus. "Oh, Trudi, I haven't seen anything so funny for a long time!" With that, he was once again laughing uncontrollably.

He had not fully recovered when the Station Master walked into the office: "What's the joke?" he asked.

"Trudi's face when you told her she was a naughty girl," said Marcus, trying not to start laughing again. "It was just so funny."

The Station Master smiled at Trudi. "Don't worry about it, lass," he said kindly. "I knew you weren't intending to be rude to me. I'd have sent you packing from the station if I'd thought that. It just reminded me of the old days." He looked a little sad. "It's a long time since I was your age, you know."

The two schoolfriends said nothing as the elderly man continued. "I'd have liked to have kids myself, you know, but it never happened."

Then he looked at Marcus and Trudi: "Anyway," he said, "Sid Parkes, Station Master and General Dogsbody, at your service. What can I do for you?"

"We wanted to know why they're closing our railway line." said Trudi boldly.

Sid whistled. "You don't ask easy questions, do you?" he said.

The old railwayman sat in silence for a moment or so, as the children watched him patiently.

"I'm an old man," he said at last. "I'm sixty-five in February and I was going to retire then but they asked me to stay on until the end of March."

"Why?" asked Marcus.

"The reason's very simple," replied Sid. "So they don't have to appoint another Station Master to replace me when I go. They want to close the station down."

"But why?" persisted Marcus.

Sid frowned, "I hardly know you," he replied. "What are your names, anyway?"

"I'm Marcus - Marcus Redlands."

"And I'm Trudi Barnes."

"Where do you live?"

The two friends told him.

"I've got one even more important question." Sid looked sharply at the other two. "Can I trust you?"

"How do you mean, Sid?" asked Marcus.

"Let me put it bluntly to you - can I be sure that you won't go blurting out everything I say outside this office?"

"You can trust us." replied Marcus solemnly.

"Trudi?"

"I won't repeat anything you don't want me to. I don't want to get you into trouble."

"Alright, then." Sid paused again, and the others wondered whether he had decided not to say anything after all. He then took up the story. "When I first came here, it was a very busy station. There were two railway tracks in use then, not just one like there is today. There seemed to be a train leaving or arriving all the time. Some were carrying passengers, like they do now, but a lot were carrying goods."

The others nodded.

"So why are there fewer trains now?" asked Marcus.

"Very simple, my young friend. Do your parents have a car?"

"My Mother has a car, yes."

Sid glanced at Trudi. "What about your parents?"

"Yes, my Dad has a car."

"She doesn't say a lot, does she?" said the Station Master, breaking off from his tale.

"I don't know," said Marcus with a grin. "She said quite a lot to me during school assembly the other day. I was very surprised."

"Ah, well, young man," continued Sid. "Them's tales out of school, and I expect she could tell as many as you could. Anyway, as I was saying, your parents have got cars, and that's nothing to be ashamed of because most people have. Trouble is, they use them these days instead of the train to get to work or go shopping or whatever."

"So not enough people are using the railway?" said Trudi.

"That's about the size of it, Miss."

"How can we change that - get people and goods back on to the railway?"

"I don't think you can, Miss. They've all discovered the freedom of their cars and businesses use vans to make their deliveries these days. You'll only persuade them to do otherwise when the roads get completely clogged up – and by then it might be too late."

"What do you mean - too late?" asked Trudi.

"I mean that by then we might not have much railway track left. It's disappearing very fast at the moment, you know."

"So somebody really ought to take a stand - try to save the Banham to Royds Well line!"

"Aye, they ought to try."

"You don't think they will be able to save it, Mr Parkes?" Marcus joined the conversation once again.

"Sid, you can call me Sid, young man," said the railwayman. "No, I don't think you'll manage to save the railway line. The company has said they will close it and they will."

"Would you like to save the line?" asked Trudi.

"This station has been my life, young lady. I'd certainly like to save it, but I don't hold out any false hopes."

"Would you help us if we started a campaign to save the railway line?" asked Marcus.

The elderly man looked sad. "I wish I could," he said. "Look, young man, I work here. The railway company pay my wages. I can't start helping people who are campaigning against the company - I'd be sacked and I'd lose my pension."

Marcus and Trudi were disappointed. If Sid couldn't help them, who could?

"Could you at least put up a poster for us?" pleaded Marcus.

Suddenly, Sid looked annoyed. "Have you not been listening to a word I've been saying, lad? This is railway property – I'd be sacked on the spot if I put a poster up here. Now I think if you're going to harass me like this, you'd both better go."

"We're sorry if we've offended you," said Trudi. "We only want to save the railway line."

"Aye, I know you do, lass." said Sid rather more gently. "Believe me, so do I - I'm sorry for getting angry like that. You can stay a few minutes more – how about some cocoa?"

The children accepted eagerly.

"Listen, you two," said the Station Master as they were sipping their drinks. "I want to save this line as much as you do, but I'm not going to lose my job to do it. If you need some advice, and I can trust you not to repeat what I say, you can come and chat with me any time you like. Do we understand each other?"

"Yes," said Marcus and Trudi in chorus.

"So how would *you* start a campaign?" asked Marcus.

Sid hesitated. "I'd first try to understand the facts," he said. "A lot of trains are running during the day with very few people on them - there's also a bus service from here to Royds Well and that probably carries more people. Why? Because it's cheaper. If your campaign gets a lot of publicity, that's what the railway company are going to say - that there's no demand for the trains and anybody who wants to will still be able to catch a bus."

"No demand for the trains?" questioned Marcus.

"You don't see many people on the trains when you're going to and from school. There are perhaps about the same number at lunchtime. In the middle of the morning and the middle of the afternoon there's hardly anybody on the train."

Marcus and Trudi were silent. They could see why the company wanted to close the line - but they desperately wanted to keep it open.

"Is there anybody we could speak to from the company?" asked Marcus.

"Philip Belstone is the Regional Director at the headquarters in Dunston." said the Station Master. "You could try speaking to him, but I'm not sure how far you'll get."

"How do we get there by train?" asked Marcus. Sid told him. Knowing that, Marcus and Trudi decided they ought to go at last.

"Listen, you two," said the Station Master as they were about to leave. "Stick up your posters in the shops around the town and get people to sign your petition. But don't forget that you might have to start answering some awkward questions, and don't expect too much."

"I like him," said Trudi, as she and Marcus walked away from the station.

"So do I," agreed Marcus. "He didn't seem too hopeful, though, did he?"

"No, he didn't. Still, that doesn't stop us trying."

"If anybody can save the railway, *we will*."

The schoolfriends walked on in silence towards the shops.

"Marcus," Trudi suddenly broke the silence. "Just one thing."

"What's that?" Marcus replied.

"Just make sure I don't have to stick my tongue out at you in front of Sid again, will you?"

They both laughed. It had been a good morning so far...

Chapter 6

A Successful Morning

The schoolfriends decided to visit the cake shop first. The little old lady behind the counter was a friend of Trudi's grandmother and the girl was sure that she would put up a poster.

"Now then, young Trudi," said Mrs Pickles as she walked through the door. "You're not going to buy all my buns and stuff yourself up while your Dad's out, are you? I shall certainly tell your grandmother if you do!"

Trudi laughed. "No, Mrs Pickles," she said. "We wondered if you could put up a poster in your window for us?"

"A poster? What's that about, then?" asked the old lady.

"About the railway. They want to close it." Trudi handed a poster to Mrs Pickles.

The lady studied it for a moment, then said, "You're planning a demonstration? I'm not sure I like the sound of that."

"Oh, it's not a real demonstration, Mrs Pickles." said Trudi quickly. "We just want a few people to gather at the town hall to show support for the railway."

"I see." The lady looked thoughtful. For an awful moment Trudi feared she was going to refuse.

"Alright," said Mrs Pickles at last. "It's for a good cause - I'll let you put up a poster in my window. I'd be sorry to see the railway disappear myself - it's been there for eighty years, you know."

"Must be nearly as old as you, Mrs Pickles," said Marcus before he could stop himself.

"Nearly as old as me, indeed." said the woman, with a twinkle in her eye. "I shall be hanging *you* in the window in a minute, never mind the poster."

Marcus blushed. "Sorry, Mrs Pickles," he said, sincerely. "I didn't mean it."

"And there was I just about to offer you a cup of cocoa and a bun," continued the lady.

Trudi's eyes lit up. "You were?"

"Yes, my dear. Do you want some?"

"Yes, please."

"Does he?" Mrs Pickles nodded at Marcus.

Trudi smiled, "Just give him bread and water. It's what he deserves."

The lady smiled at Marcus. "I shall be kinder than Trudi, even if you were rude to me."

"Thank you, Mrs Pickles."

It was just after nine o'clock that morning and there was nobody else in the shop so the three sat in the back and enjoyed their cocoa. The old lady had never met Marcus before, so she asked him to tell her all about himself – where he lived, what he enjoyed doing at school and half a dozen other things.

"There's not much Mrs Pickles doesn't know about me now," grumbled Marcus when they had left the shop half an hour or so later. "It was like being interrogated by the Headmistress! I hope they don't all offer us cocoa and buns - we won't be back by lunchtime if they do."

"She's lovely though, isn't she?" said Trudi and Marcus agreed.

Their next call was to the hardware shop, where an earnest young man with glasses was standing behind the counter.

"Would you put this up for us, please?" asked Marcus, waving the poster.

"Certainly will," replied the man with a grin. "Two of my best customers use the train from Royds Well to get here - they reckon there isn't a shop like it there. I'll join your demonstration, too - when is it, Wednesday lunchtime?"

"It is. One o'clock."

"See you there."

Marcus almost skipped out of the shop. "That was successful, anyway," he said. "He even said he would attend the demonstration."

The two friends managed to place seven of their posters in shop windows and decided to call in at the Baker's to see if he would put the last one in his window. It was to be their first disappointment of the morning.

"I'm not into politics and all that stuff," said the somewhat miserable-looking man behind the counter. "You lose your friends that way."

Looking at the man, Marcus was surprised that he had any.

"Anyway," continued the Baker unhelpfully, "if the railway company says it's going to close that line, it will close it and there's nothing you or I can do about it."

"Thanks anyway," said Marcus, not entirely sure what he was thanking the Baker for.

"What do we do with the last poster, then?" he asked Trudi when they were back in the street.

Just at that moment Trudi spotted the office of the local newspaper, 'The Banham Recorder.'

Marcus looked in the same direction. "Good idea."

They called into the office, asking the lady behind the counter if she would put up the poster for them.

"I'll have to ask Mark - he's the reporter here." She buzzed him on the internal telephone.

"I'll be straight down," said a voice at the other end, after the lady had explained what the friends wanted.

Mark rushed down the wooden stairs. "Hello," he greeted Marcus and Trudi warmly, and shook hands with them as if they were old friends. He gripped their hands so tightly that Trudi's hurt a little when he had let it go. "What can I do for you?"

They explained about the railway line and showed the poster to the young reporter.

"Demonstration as well?" he said with a gleam in his eye. "Yes, of course you can put a poster up here. Do you mind if I send a photographer to take your pictures on Wednesday?"

"Please do," replied Marcus enthusiastically.

"Right," said the reporter. "I'll stick it up this minute and it won't be forgotten. We want as many people as possible to turn up, don't we?"

This was marvellous and somewhat unexpected - the journalist might have been talking about his own campaign. He was sure to give the demonstration a good write-up.

"Have you thought about having a few banners at the demonstration?" asked Mark.

"Banners?" asked Marcus, surprised.

"Yes, you know, you could have a placard reading ROYDS WELL HIGH PUPILS SAY NO TO RAILWAY CLOSURE - that sort of thing. I presume you go to Royds Well High?"

"We do." replied Trudi.

"Are you sure the school would like it?" asked Marcus, nervously.

"If anybody from there sees it, they'll love it," said the reporter enthusiastically. "It shows pupils from the school taking part in the wider community. It will also help to make sure that the story gets into the paper. We're printed in Royds Well, you see - a banner like that would mean they would put it in the *'Royds Well Recorder'* too. That would give you plenty of publicity."

"Trust me." he said as the two friends looked dubious.

"Oh, why not!" exclaimed Marcus after a pause.

"Good man!" said the reporter. "We'll save the railway yet."

It was now mid-morning. Marcus didn't want to go home yet, so he asked: "Do you fancy a drink in the cafe? I'll treat you."

"You're on," replied Trudi.

Whilst drinking some more cocoa, the two friends discussed their morning's work.

"I think we've done really well," said Trudi. "We've left all the posters and only one person turned us down."

"Yes, that miserable Baker," said Marcus. "I shouldn't think he's got many friends left to lose."

Trudi giggled, "He didn't make any new ones this morning, anyway."

"Some very surprising people agreed to put our posters up."

"Yes. I was very surprised the hardware man did. Even more surprised when the journalist did."

"Funny chap, that journalist. He seemed to be on our side, though. Do you think we should do a banner?"

"I suppose we could," replied Trudi. "He seemed to think it would help us - and that we wouldn't get into trouble for it. Yes – let's."

"I feel we're really doing something about this railway now. It's fun, too."

"Better than school, anyway," said Trudi, words which, until a few days ago, Marcus would never have expected to hear from her.

"Now, now - that word is banned during the holidays."

"So when do we do the banners, then?"

"How about my place after lunch, say two o'clock."

"So I can make peace with your Mother - alright, Marcus."

He laughed. "Just try not to impress her too much, Trudi. I want her to allow my other friends to visit me too."

When Trudi returned home, she was surprised to find her grandmother there.

"Gran – I didn't expect to see you here."

"Aren't you pleased to see your old grandmother?"

"Of course I am." Trudi gave her a hug.

Trudi sat down at the dining table while her grandmother remained standing, apparently in deep thought.

"Trudi." There was a serious tone in the older lady's voice.

"Yes, Gran?"

"I went into the cake shop today. Mrs Pickles, you know."

Trudi said nothing. She had a feeling she knew what would follow.

"I gather you were there earlier this morning?"

"Yes, with Marcus Redlands. He's a boy in my class."

"Yes. You had some free cake and cocoa."

"Mrs Pickles offered them to us. We thought it was very kind."

"So it was. You also left a poster."

Trudi felt as if a bolt of electricity had passed through her.

"We did." Trudi was silent for a moment, before asking, "You didn't ask her to take it down?"

"No! No, of course not." Gran smiled, then looked more serious again. "I just wondered what it was about."

"We want to save the railway line to Royds Well - the railway company wants to close it."

"So I gather. You're organising a demonstration?"

"I… suppose we are. We just want a few people to stand on the steps of the town hall and protest, really."

"Does your Father know anything about this?"

"I shouldn't think he does. They only stuck a notice up on Friday announcing the closure."

Gran sounded mildly impatient, "I meant, Trudi, does he know about your campaign?"

"No."

"Do you think he would approve?"

Trudi smiled. "Who knows?"

"You're not going to get yourself into trouble over this?"

"We know what we're doing, Gran." said Trudi, though she was beginning to have doubts.

"Then your interfering old Grandmother will say no more about it." said Gran, smiling.

Trudi gave her a big hug. "I've never thought of you as an interfering old Grandmother," she said. Then she looked more serious. "You won't tell Dad, will you?"

"No," Gran gave a sigh. "No, I won't tell him, but I'm still not convinced that you shouldn't."

Her grandmother went into the sitting room whilst Trudi remained where she was, thinking hard.

'Should I tell Dad?' she thought.

The answer to that was probably "yes," but she was not sure that he would understand. For the moment she would say nothing – and hope against hope that he didn't find out...

Chapter 7

A Little Demonstration

Trudi woke up on Wednesday morning feeling a tremendous sense of excitement. She was going to be doing something today, but she couldn't quite remember what.

Then it came to her - of course! It was the day of the demonstration. She and Marcus had made banners for it as the reporter had suggested:

ROYDS WELL HIGH PUPILS SAY NO TO RAILWAY CLOSURE

She hoped that it would make a good photograph in the newspaper.

As the morning wore on, Trudi began to have doubts. How many people would turn up at the demonstration? Would it achieve anything?

They might get a few more signatures for their petition of course, but a demonstration attended by very few people would not be helpful. It might suggest to the railway company that not many people cared.

Still, she decided, it was too late to worry about that now. They had advertised a demonstration outside the town hall at half-past one and they were going to have one. After all, the press would be there.

At least the press seemed to be on the side of the railway, thought Trudi. That might prove to be useful…

At one o'clock, having eaten a light lunch, Trudi put on her jeans, a baggy sweater, a scarf and her oldest coat.

"You do look a scruff, dear," said Gran as she was about to leave. "Are you going to that demonstration?"

"I am," replied Trudi. She hoped that Marcus would remember to bring the banners they had spent so long making. The two friends met at about ten-past one outside the town hall, noting that nobody else appeared to be there.

Marcus glanced nervously at his watch. "We're going to look real idiots if nobody turns up."

"We've got twenty minutes," replied Trudi, trying to sound reassuring. She had never organised a demonstration before.

The man from the hardware shop arrived ten minutes later.

"Are we all there is?" he asked.

"So far," replied Marcus.

A couple of minutes later, a well-dressed young man joined them.

"Is this the demonstration?" he asked. "I'm a local solicitor but I'm very keen to save the railway, you know. I spend most of my spare time on trains."

"Four." Marcus realised, to his embarrassment, that he was counting out loud.

A scruffily dressed young man with a black and white dog was the next to arrive. By half-past one there were perhaps a dozen people, including a pair of elderly ladies who had walked up to the group to ask what was going on. Marcus could only presume that, since they had not walked away again, they were supporters.

As the town hall clock struck half-past one, Marcus realised that the idea of a demonstration had been a total disaster. The journalist from 'The Banham Recorder' would be turning up any minute to witness this humiliation. He wasn't quite sure what he should do, but he couldn't just stand there.

Passing the banner to the solicitor - who looked a little old to be sporting the slogan 'Royds Well High Pupils Say No To Railway Closure' - he stood nervously in front of the crowd.

"We all know why we're here," he shouted. "We're here today because we want to tell the railway company that we don't want them to close the line to

Royds Well - in fact, we're going to make sure they don't close it."

A cheer came from the crowd - as much of a cheer as crowd of a dozen people could manage.

"So let's show them," called Marcus, beginning to enjoy playing the part of rabble-rouser. "WHAT DO WE WANT?"

"TO STOP THE RAILWAY CLOSURE," shouted back the crowd. Trudi and the solicitor were waving their banners, the two old ladies shook their umbrellas and the man with the dog waved his fist.

"WHEN DO WE WANT IT?" shouted Marcus, thinking back to demonstrations he had seen on the television news.

"NOW," called back the crowd, who must have watched the same television programmes.

"So our message to the railway company is quite simple," said Marcus. "We're not going to let them shut the line down – we're going to save the railway!" There were more cheers.

At this moment, the journalist whom Marcus and Trudi had met the previous Monday rushed up along with a photographer. They were soon joined by a cameraman from the regional television station. Marcus joined Trudi and stood holding a banner along with the rest of the crowd as the photographer took pictures, including one of them on their own.

The reporter then asked Marcus and Trudi to explain in their own words why they were protesting and asked them a few questions.

The final question to Marcus was: "You have been carrying a banner saying that your school is against the closure of the railway line. Are you sure that the other pupils at Royds Well High agree with you?"

He replied without hesitation, "Yes I am sure the pupils at Royds Well High School support our campaign."

"Thank you very much." said the journalist, who then left with the photographer.

The cameraman, who had said nothing until now, asked if the crowd would chant a few slogans for the benefit of the television audience, "just so they know what it's about."

Marcus stood in front of the crowd again, this time holding his banner, and he and the other supporters of the railway line repeated the ritual they had engaged in before the arrival of the press - the speech and the chanting.

The cameraman also spoke to one or two members of the crowd, including the solicitor and one of the old ladies.

Marcus and Trudi were very disappointed that they were not interviewed, since they had organised the protest. The cameraman disappeared and the demonstrators began to melt away. By two o'clock Marcus and Trudi were once more on their own.

"What do you think?" asked Marcus.

"I was disappointed that more people didn't turn up," replied Trudi, "but at least there were a dozen or so of us. We'll have to see what it looks like on television and in the newspaper."

Trudi was looking forward to sitting down with Gran to watch the regional news programme at six o'clock, but that did not go according to plan. Her Father was often not back home from work until eight in the evening, but that day he returned to the house at half-past five.

"Evening, Trudi. Evening, Mother," he said cheerily. "I'll just change out of my suit and then I might look at the news in a few minutes. I don't often get the chance to see it."

Trudi was horrified. "You can't let him watch the regional news," she said to her grandmother after her Father had disappeared upstairs. "The piece about the railway might be on it. He'll kill me if he finds out I've been involved in a demonstration."

Gran looked worried. "I did try to warn you, dear," she said. "I'll see what I can do, but if your Father is determined to watch it, there's not much I can do. He'll find out about it soon enough if the television cameras were there."

Trudi knew this, but she wanted to keep the secret from her Father for as long as possible.

Mr Barnes came back into the sitting room, switched on the television set and sat down in an armchair.

"This is delightful," he said. "I wish I was home at this time every night."

Trudi would have been very happy to see her Father return home early on any other evening but this one.

Mr Barnes watched the national news. The regional news followed it. The fight to save the railway was not the main story, but it was mentioned in the introduction. Fortunately the pictures which were shown were of the railway itself, not of the demonstration.

After a few minutes, but before the piece about the railway line, Gran turned to Trudi's Father, "I had an idea about your Christmas present the other day. Shall we discuss it?"

"By all means," said Mr Barnes. "What was your idea?"

"Oh, I can't discuss it here," said Gran. She added, half whispering: "I've got an idea for her present as well."

"Must we discuss it now?" asked Trudi's Father wearily. "Christmas is about two months away."

"I thought I'd mention it while it was in my mind. As I say, if we can talk about it away from prying ears."

"Alright," sighed Mr Barnes. "You win Mother."

So Gran and her Father went into another room. Trudi, who had to admire her grandmother's persistence, breathed a sigh of relief. Despite her curiosity, she switched the television set off. She didn't want the others coming back into the room while the piece about the railway was being shown.

Meanwhile Marcus was watching the regional news on television at home. Fortunately, his Mother was out. The first few items on the programme seemed quite dull, but at last it moved on to the piece about the railway line.

"Two local schoolchildren are determined to save the railway line from Banham to Royds Well," said the television presenter. "Here's our transport correspondent John Barlow."

"The railway company announced only a few days ago that it intends to close the branch line from Banham to Royds Well," said the transport correspondent, as the screen showed pictures of a steam train travelling on the line. "Now, two children, Trudi Barnes and Marcus Redlands from Royds Well High School, say that they are determined to stop the closure."

The screen now showed Marcus and Trudi speaking about the railway line. The cameraman must have been filming while the journalist was talking to them, but only the answers were shown, not the questions.

The final comment shown was from Marcus, "The pupils at Royds Well High School support our campaign."

"Whether or not they do," continued the transport correspondent, "the demonstration today only attracted about a dozen people."

The screen was now showing the crowd, with Marcus addressing them. With all the waving of banners, umbrellas and fists, they looked quite ridiculous.

"They are going to need a lot more people if they are going to persuade the railway company to change its mind," the report- concluded. "Now back to Mary Jennings in the studio."

"We did try to get hold of a spokesman for the railway but they weren't available for comment," said Mary Jennings. "And now sport…"

Marcus switched off the television.

At first, he had felt that the report had been helpful. He and Trudi had both spoken well, though he would have preferred it if they had shown the questions as well as the answers.

Of course, as these had been asked by the newspaper reporter and not their own correspondent, it had been necessary to edit them out.

He was a little concerned about the final comment he had made – "The pupils at Royds Well High School support our campaign." That had been in answer to a question and Marcus recalled that he had said something like 'Yes I am sure the pupils of Royds Well High School support our campaign.' Since he had not had the opportunity to speak to any of his classmates about the railway, let alone any of the other pupils at school, that might have sounded a little better if any of the teachers, or even the other pupils, had happened to be watching.

Still, they probably weren't…

The demonstration had looked idiotic. Marcus could only hope that viewers had not paid too much attention to that either. All in all, Marcus now had serious doubts about whether the demonstration had been a good idea. He hoped that he would feel happier when he had seen the local newspaper the following Friday…

Chapter 8

Mr Belstone

'*The Banham Recorder*' was not delivered to Marcus' home, so he slipped out to buy a copy on Friday morning. A copy of the paper was delivered to Trudi's house. Fortunately it arrived after her Father had gone to work. Both Marcus and Trudi were pleased to see that the story about the railway was the major item on the front page...

Next to it was a picture of the demonstrators, in which Marcus and Trudi could be seen clearly carrying their banners. Beneath that picture were two smaller portraits of the schoolfriends. Each of the friends was happy with the story, written by Mark Richards, the journalist they had met the other day.

'Pupils at Royds Well High support us'

FIGHT AGAINST RAIL CLOSURE

The Railway Company announced the closure of the Banham to Royds Well Branch line late last week after the "Recorder" went to press. No reason has been given for this and this newspaper has been unable to speak to the company. We understand, however, that passenger numbers have dropped very substantially over the last ten years and are continuing to do so. Railway lines all over the country have been closing for this reason.

Royds Well High School pupils Trudi Barnes and Marcus Redlands are determined to stop the closure of their line, however. They have travelled to school on the train from Banham for the past year and cannot imagine their town without the railway. They urged residents of the town to write to the Regional Director, Philip Belstone, at his head-quarters.

(The newspaper helpfully printed his address and telephone number).

Marcus Redlands told our reporter: "the pupils of Royds Well High School support our campaign."

-

The article also pointed out that services on the line from Royds Well to Dunston, which was in the opposite direction from Banham, would not be affected. Yes, Marcus and Trudi thought as they read the article carefully, that piece could do their campaign no harm at all…

Trudi's only problem was to make sure that her Father didn't read about the campaign. She took the cover of that week's newspaper, putting it safely in her bedroom, and replaced it with the cover of the previous week's, throwing the rest of that newspaper in the dustbin.

She told her grandmother what she had done.

"We'll just have to hope your Father assumes they have made a mistake and reprinted the front and back pages from last week." said Gran.

Trudi now regarded the older lady as one of the most loyal supporters of the campaign, even though she had not been on the demonstration and they had not actually discussed the closure of the railway line.

Trudi hoped that her grandmother was right – and, above all, that her Father wouldn't slip out and buy a second copy of the newspaper...

Marcus was expecting his cousin Stephen to visit at about eleven o'clock that morning and he had an idea. Stephen was sixteen - four years older than Marcus - and he spoke very self-confidently. If he were to telephone the Regional Director of the railway, perhaps they could make an appointment to see the man. Certainly Marcus' cousin seemed to be able to talk himself into - and out of - a lot of situations…

Marcus told his cousin about the railway and Stephen was very happy to help. He picked up the phone and dialled the number.

"Excuse me," he said smoothly. "Could I speak to Philip Belstone, please?"

"Who is it?" asked the voice at the other end of the line.

"Stephen Redman. I don't suppose he knows me." Marcus' cousin would have been very surprised if he did.

Marcus noted his cousin had made a slight alteration to his surname when giving it to the person at the other end of the line. Presumably he thought that the railway director might have seen the name 'Redlands' in the newspaper or heard it on television when the demonstration was reported.

"It's about the closure of the line from Banham to Royds Well."

A moment later another voice spoke to Stephen. "Philip Belstone here, Regional Director of the Railways. What can I do to help?"

"Stephen Redman here. I've just been reading about the closure of the line from Banham to Royds Well.

I've got some ideas - I wondered if we could have a chat sometime."

"We certainly can have a chat." The voice on the other end of the line sounded much more cheerful now. "Do you know I've been answering calls all morning about that - there was an awful article about it in the '*Royds Well Recorder*' this morning by some fellow called Richards. Evidently some interfering kids are trying to whip up public feeling about it," Mr Belstone said. "Yes, I'll speak to anybody who has ideas about it - just as long as you're not one of these dreadful protesters!"

Stephen coughed and said that he wasn't.

"Half past three this afternoon?"

"That will be fine. There may be three of us."

"The more the merrier." he answered.

When he had hung up at the end of the conversation, Stephen repeated it to Marcus.

Marcus whistled, "I thought it was a good piece," he said. "Evidently it's got the railway company rattled - that *is* good news."

"We've arranged a meeting with him anyway," said Stephen cautiously. "Don't get your hopes up too high, Marcus, we still don't know what he'll say. I think it's unlikely he'll change his mind."

Marcus was just delighted with what Stephen had arranged. He telephoned Trudi, who was free to go with them. They discussed the newspaper article and agreed that Mark Richards had done a good job for them. Marcus had no sooner put the phone down than it rang again. This time it was the journalist.

"Did you like my story?" he asked.

"It was great," Marcus replied.

"My editor thought so too," said Mark Richards. "It was on the front page of the '*Royds Well Recorder*' too - a lot more people read that. I wondered - would you like to write a letter to the editor? You could thank the paper for running the story and put a few more arguments for saving the line - keep it in the news."

"Good idea," replied Marcus.

He telephoned Trudi again and a few minutes later she arrived at his house. Soon, with the help of a few ideas from the others, she had drafted a letter to the newspaper.

"Excellent letter." said Stephen. Trudi was pleased.

The trio walked to the newspaper office to hand it in. Mark Richards came downstairs to see them and read it.

"Wonderful," he said. "I notice you've only put your names at the bottom of the page. Would you like to add the name of the school?"

Trudi borrowed the journalist's pen and wrote very neatly 'Royds Well High School'.

"That man is really helpful," said Trudi as they left the newspaper office. "He couldn't say so in the article, of course, but I think he's on our side."

"I'm sure he is." Marcus agreed.

The three arranged to meet again at half past one at Banham station, from where they took the train to Royds Well before changing for Dunston. All three were smartly dressed for the occasion.

Trudi was wearing her best dress (which Marcus remembered seeing on a very wet evening!) and the two boys were wearing smart pullovers and ties.

Climbing on to the train from Banham, Marcus took care not to kick Trudi's heel on this occasion! The friends noticed that there were very few passengers on it. The railway company certainly had a strong argument for closing the line, thought Trudi gloomily.

The ride from Royds Well took three quarters of an hour and this time the train was pulled by a much faster (but much less interesting) diesel. At last, they were in Dunston and the offices of the railway company were just next to the station. There was half an hour to spare, so Stephen, Marcus and Trudi went into the station cafe.

Ten minutes before their appointment, they walked into the plush offices of the railway company.

"Stephen Redman," said Marcus' cousin very confidently at the reception desk. "My friends and I have an appointment with Mr Belstone at half-past three."

"Right, sir," said the pleasant young woman behind the counter. "I'll just let him know you're here." She spoke to Mr Belstone on the telephone.

"You're to go up on the lift," said the young woman after putting the telephone down. "It's the fifth floor - he'll meet you there."

Each of them felt a little nervous as they travelled to the fifth floor. Mr Belstone hadn't sounded very sympathetic to the campaign to save the railway when he spoke to Stephen on the telephone, so what would he be like now, face to face?

Philip Belstone was a tall, slender man with greying hair, they noted as the lift doors opened, perhaps in his early fifties. His smile turned to a look of astonishment when he saw the three friends.

"Stephen Redman?" he asked.

"Stephen Redlands," corrected Marcus' cousin. Now that they were meeting the Regional Director, there was no need to use a false name.

"You'd better follow me," said the Railway Director blankly. Once they were in his office, he shut the door behind them.

"I don't need any introduction to your friends," he said quietly. "You're Trudi Barnes and Marcus

Redlands, aren't you? You must excuse me - I have a telephone call to make."

He disappeared through another door which had a large glass panel.

"You stupid idiot, Wendy." The three rather embarrassed youngsters could hear every word Mr Belstone was saying - he was obviously telling off the poor young lady at reception. "You've sent a bunch of kids upstairs to see me! Do you think I've got time in my busy day to see kids? They're the idiots who want to save the line," he yelled. "No doubt they'll tell me some sob-story about how they can't get to school."

There was a pause, then the boss shouted even more loudly, "Next time you do that, young lady, you'll be out of a job!" He slammed the phone down.

Trudi was horrified. The young receptionist had been so pleasant to the friends - she did not deserve to be treated like that by this hateful man.

Stephen was angry. The receptionist had simply told her boss that the youngsters had arrived - he had made the appointment. Stephen was aware that he had slightly changed his surname to get to see Mr Belstone - but that was not the young lady's fault. How dare Mr Belstone speak to his employee like that?

Marcus' cousin was tempted to say something to the bully when he came back into the room, but he bit his lip. The young woman, after all, would still be working with Mr Belstone after the friends had left the building. Anything he said might make matters worse.

"Well, Stephen," said the Railway Director, closing the glass door behind him. "As I said, I don't need any introduction from your friends, they're the two troublemakers who have plastered themselves over the '*Royds Well Recorder*' in their attempt to save the railway. I was under the impression when I spoke to you this morning that you were some businessman who might want to buy the railway and that's why I agreed to talk to you. I must congratulate you on getting to see me under false pretences."

Stephen said nothing. This did not seem to be much of a compliment…

"Since you're not going to make any such offer," the Railway Director continued, "I'm not going to waste any more time with you, except to say that your journalist friend did me a favour. A company got in touch with me not an hour ago to say that they are interested in buying the station, so that they can knock it down and build one of these new supermarkets on it."

He looked with pleasure at the distressed faces of the three visitors.

"You're joking," said Stephen bitterly.

"No, I'm not," smiled the Director, "and once that's signed and sealed, there'll be no question of saving the

Banham line. The sooner that deal goes through the better as far as I am concerned!"

The others said nothing. They had been so confident about their campaign this morning. Now it seemed as if they might already be too late...

Chapter 9

Another Meeting

"Anyway," continued Mr Belstone, "as I say, we won't waste any more time here. I'll escort you out of the building, just to make sure you don't get any silly ideas about wandering around."

So Marcus, Trudi and Stephen marched towards the lift, feeling like prisoners with the Railway Director as their guard.

When they got to the ground floor, Mr Belstone followed them out of the lift.

"Take a good look at these faces, Wendy." He shouted to the young lady at reception. "Next time you let them in, you'll be leaving with them."

He drew closer to the receptionist and noticed as the others did, that her eyes were red. She had been crying.

"Oh, turn the tap off, you stupid woman," he said. "I can trust you to see these three off the premises, can I?"

"Yes, sir." replied Wendy faintly.

Mr Belstone disappeared.

"Can you sign the visitors' book, please?" asked the young woman. She was shaking.

"Of course." said Stephen. He took the book and Trudi took the young woman's hand and squeezed it.

"We're very sorry for getting you into trouble," she said. "We just thought if we could talk to the man in charge, he might change his mind."

There were still tears in her eyes but Wendy managed a faint smile. "It's not your fault," she said. "You're just trying to save the railway. I wish I could do something to help."

"You mustn't do anything that might cause you to lose your job," said Stephen. "Trudi's right, we feel awful about the way he treated you. He's just a hateful, nasty man - but I shouldn't have pretended to be an adult and arranged to meet him."

"Don't worry," repeated Wendy. "I've no hard feelings against you. I just wish I could help you stop them closing the railway."

"I suppose we shouldn't ask this," said Stephen, "but Mr Belstone said that a supermarket was interested in buying the station building in Banham, so that they can demolish it. Is that true?"

"If the boss told you that, I'm not giving away any secrets, am I? Yes, somebody from a supermarket company spoke to him this afternoon, but I don't think they'd be ready to agree to buy the land for quite a while."

"Why not?" asked Stephen.

"Because they would need planning permission for the store. They won't buy the land until they have got that."

"So, we have some time yet?" asked Trudi.

"Yes, but don't waste any time." The young woman seemed to have quite recovered now, and Trudi realised she was still touching her hand. She let go.

"What's your name?" Wendy asked her.

"Trudi - Trudi Barnes."

"Write down your address and telephone number on this piece of paper," said Wendy, "in case I can help you." Trudi did as she was asked.

The phone buzzed on the desk at reception. Wendy picked it up. "Yes, they've gone." she said, and put the receiver down.

"You'd better go now." said Wendy. "Have you all signed the book? No, Trudi, you haven't - could you just do that for me?" Trudi obliged and signed the book then she and the others left hastily.

"What a nasty man!" exclaimed Stephen when they were on the train back to Royds Well.

"Wasn't he," said Trudi, "and Wendy is such a lovely young woman too, I don't know how she can put up with him."

"One thing about it," said Marcus. "That man doesn't like our involvement in this campaign and it sounds as if a lot of people have been complaining to him about the closure. It sounds as if we're winning."

"Don't be too hasty, Marcus." replied his cousin. "If the railway company sells that station, we're done for."

"Like Wendy said, we'd better not waste any time." said Trudi.

They rode back to Royds Well in silence, wondering what they should do next. Then they sat on one of the seats at the station, watching as the steam train, that would take back to Banham, arrived.

"I can see why you want to save it," said Stephen. "That engine is gorgeous, isn't it?"

"Isn't it just?" agreed Marcus. "Just look at those brown and white carriages too - you don't see many trains like that nowadays."

They stood gazing at the train from the platform until it was almost time for it to leave.

"I hope I'm still riding home on this in six months' time." murmured Trudi as they climbed into the carriage.

"Is there anybody else you could talk to?" asked Stephen.

"I can't think of anybody," replied Marcus.

"What about the local MP?" asked Trudi.

"We could try him," replied Marcus. "Elderly fellow called George Scott, isn't he? I think my Mother once wrote to him about something."

"Was he helpful?" asked Trudi enthusiastically.

"I don't think she ever commented."

The trio returned to Marcus' house and looked at the local newspaper. It appeared that the MP, George Scott, would be holding a surgery that evening at the Town Hall at six o'clock.

"I'll let you two go on your own this time," said Stephen, who was staying overnight at Marcus' house. "I can't say that I was very successful with Mr Belstone."

"It wasn't your fault," protested Trudi. "He was just a nasty man."

"Even so, I'll leave this one to you."

Trudi and Marcus arrived at the Town Hall in Banham just as the clock was about to strike six. Already a couple of older ladies were waiting to see George Scott.

The MP invited people who were seeing him into a private room, and it was almost three-quarters of an hour before the second lady came out and it was their turn.

George Scott must have been in his late fifties. He was mainly bald, with a little grey hair, and wore spectacles. He was a tall, well-built man, and he smiled as he invited Marcus and Trudi into the private room.

"What can I do for you kids?" he asked.

Marcus groaned inwardly. He was already fairly sure that George Scott wasn't going to take the opinions of 'kids' seriously.

"We've come about the railway," Trudi began. "The railway company want to close down the line between Royds Well and Banham. We travel to school on that line every day..."

"Then you'll be bound to miss it." cut in the MP sympathetically and making as if to stand up.

"Oh, we're not going to give up hope yet," continued Trudi. "We've started a campaign to save the line - we wanted to ask for your support."

"I quite agree with you, I think it's a shame," replied the MP. "You know, when I was a boy, and I'm not telling you when that was," he laughed, "that was a very busy station. There were two railway lines and passenger and freight trains were coming and going all day. Now, it seems as if there isn't even enough demand for one line, with trains to and from Royds Well every hour and twenty minutes. Great pity, great pity."

"People still need to get to Royds Well though." argued Trudi.

"I agree, but you see, everybody has got cars nowadays, that's why there are so few passengers on the railway and why the company is closing the line."

Trudi was feeling very annoyed by these remarks, but she was determined not to lose her temper.

"How many more cars and vans can the roads take before they become clogged up?" she asked.

George Scott laughed, "Oh, I think you can leave the planners and the politicians to worry about that," he answered. "The roads are not clogged up at the moment."

"But they will be one day," threw in Trudi, clinging on to this argument like a dog with a bone.

The MP laughed again, slightly nervously this time.

"You're an earnest little girl, aren't you?" he said, "You've almost got me worried that you are after my job!"

Trudi bit her lip and said nothing. She was furious at this man for calling her a 'little girl' and was tempted to tell him that she could no doubt do his job better than he could. None of that, however, would help.

"Well," began the MP, "if there's nothing else…"

"You're a member of the Government Party, aren't you?" The terrier had picked up a new bone.

"I certainly am," replied George Scott.

"So you could speak to Government Ministers - see if they could help save that railway line. You might even have some influence with the railway company - isn't it worth at least trying to do something?"

"My dear young lady, all this must seem very simple to you. I'm afraid the railway company can't afford to run trains all day with nobody on them. My talking to anybody won't change that."

"They're not running trains with nobody on them!" Trudi exclaimed.

"So how many people are on them?" he asked.

Trudi was silent for a moment. She did not like to reply - *'not very many'*.

"Anyway," she opened a new argument, "not everybody has a car."

"Most people do, young lady. Do you know, under this Government…"

Trudi took a deep breath and shut her eyes momentarily. She was most definitely NOT interested in a lot of statistics about car ownership.

"Of course, for those who haven't got a car, there'll still be the bus service." the MP concluded.

"The train can carry a lot more people than a bus," Trudi argued. "Anyway, it's such a lovely steam train…"

"Well, don't get all dewy-eyed about that," replied the MP. "You do realise that even if the railway company didn't close that line, they would be running diesels on it within the next couple of years? Steam engines are going to disappear."

"What?" Marcus opened his mouth for the first time since they had been in the MP 's company.

"Oh, yes." said the MP, feeling for the first time that he was actually winning this argument. "Even if you saved the line, and it's not likely that you will, you're going to have diesels running on it. That lovely steam train of yours will be scrapped, like the rest of them."

"They can't!" Marcus almost shouted.

"They can and they will," replied George Scott solemnly. "So if I were you, I would forget all about the railway. It's doomed anyway. Ride your bikes, enjoy yourselves, you don't need to worry about such things at your age."

He stood up and this time, the others did the same.

"Thank you very much for your time," said Trudi politely. "I can assure you, Mr Scott, that we intend to continue our fight to save the railway. We are sorry that you can't support us."

The MP laughed, "Don't take everything so seriously." he said, patting Trudi on the head.

When they had left the Town Hall and were well on their way back to Marcus' house, the boy burst into uncontrollable laughter.

"What's so funny?" asked Trudi, annoyed.

"Your face," Marcus laughed. "It was an absolute picture. You should have seen yourself, I expected steam to come out of your ears!"

"I didn't find it funny," replied Trudi. "It was a complete disaster. That man wouldn't lift a finger for us."

Then Trudi saw the funny side too. The two were almost helpless with laughter by the time they got back to Marcus' house.

Stephen told them that Trudi's grandmother had telephoned half an hour previously. "She wondered where you were - said you'd promised to be home at half-past six and she had a meal ready for you."

So Trudi telephoned, apologised solemnly and realised to her relief that her Father wasn't home. She was giggling again when she put down the receiver.

They weren't beaten yet...

Chapter 10

Mr Barnes Receives a Letter

"What on earth is that?"

Trudi's Father angrily tossed a letter, which he had just been reading, in front of her. Trudi froze when she saw the heading on the letter and began to read it with horror:

ROYDS WELL HIGH SCHOOL
(Headmistress: Mrs J.P. Hampshire).

Dear Mr Barnes

It has always been the policy of myself, my staff and the Governors of this School that the name of the School should not be linked with matters of politics of any kind.

It is therefore a matter of great concern to me that your daughter Trudi and another pupil should have used the name of Royds Well High School in their campaign to save a local railway line. Not content with parading the name of this School on banners, which were shown on the regional television news programme as well as on the front page of the Royds Well

Recorder, they have also presumed to tell the media that other pupils are behind their campaign.

I am unfortunately away from school on Monday and I must ask Trudi (as I shall be asking the other pupil concerned) not to attend school on that day either. I would ask you to make every effort to attend the school at ten o'clock on Tuesday morning, with Trudi, so that we can discuss your daughter's future here.

In the meantime I am sure you will impress on Trudi the importance of taking no further action in this campaign, which the newspapers and television would no doubt link to the school. I look forward to meeting you on Tuesday.

Yours sincerely
Mrs J.P. Hampshire

"I think you had better tell me what this letter is about." said Mr Barnes, very quietly and calmly.

Trudi said nothing. She was shaking. She had been so convinced that she could keep this campaign away from her Father in case he did not approve. Now he had found out - in the worst possible way. She didn't know how to begin...

Mr Barnes drummed his fingers on the table impatiently. "I'm waiting."

"Shall we go into the sitting room?" asked Trudi, wearily. "It's more comfortable there. This might take some time."

"I've got all the time in the world," replied her father coolly.

So they sat down in the sitting room. Trudi looked shame-faced. Her Father waited.

She drew a deep breath. "On the last day of the half term, another pupil and I…"

"Marcus, presumably," her Father interrupted.

She nodded. "As I was saying, we were catching the train to Royds Well when we saw a notice saying that the railway company intended to close the line. We weren't happy about that, so we decided to save it."

"I presume that you haven't managed to save it yet," said her Father. "What exactly have you done?"

"Put posters around the town and organised a demonstration outside the Town Hall."

"So that's why you wanted the poster-sized paper? When was the demonstration?"

"Wednesday lunchtime."

"And it was on the local news in the evening, which I would have seen if your Grandmother hadn't wanted to talk about Christmas presents. What does she know about this?"

Trudi was silent.

"Well?"

"Marcus and I were the only ones involved in this."

"You kept this a secret from me deliberately, didn't you?"

"I didn't think you'd understand."

"I don't. What matters to me, Trudi, is that you get a good education. Royds Well is a good school. If they stop the trains, you can go by bus."

"Trains can carry a lot of people, Dad. If we rip up the lines, we're not going to be able to use them in the future and we might find that the roads become totally clogged up."

"Don't start lecturing me, young lady. You're in very serious bother at school. You're to promise me that you will take no further part in this ridiculous campaign." There was silence.

"You don't leave this house until I have that promise."

Trudi said nothing. She was not going to make a promise which she had no intention of keeping.

"I suppose that's why I haven't seen the front page of this week's '*Banham Recorder*'. I expect your photograph was on that too."

Trudi rushed upstairs to fetch the missing front page. She was glad to leave the sitting room even for a few seconds. Mr Barnes read the article.

"Why did you have to mention the name of the School and stick it on your banners?" he asked. "If you hadn't done that, nobody could have objected. I suppose this is the same piece Mrs Hampshire has seen in the '*Royds Well Recorder*'?"

"I presume so," replied Trudi. "I haven't seen a copy of that."

"I don't suppose it's very often that a reporter from here gets on the front page of the Royds Well edition of the *Recorder*," snorted her Father. "He must be very pleased with himself."

Normally, Trudi would have defended the reporter - after all, he had been a good friend of the campaign. She decided that this was not the moment to speak out.

"I'm going to speak to Marcus' parents about this," said Mr Barnes. "Are they on the telephone?"

"He lives with his Mother - his Father is dead. They have a telephone, yes."

"Then perhaps you would be good enough to stir yourself and let me have it?"

Trudi hesitated. Should she give the number to her Father when he was in such a foul mood? Might that not just create trouble between the two families?

"I'm waiting."

There was no point in resisting, Trudi's Father had decided what he was going to do. Explanations, if any were needed, would have to be made later.

Trudi found the number and gave it to him.

"I'll speak to Marcus' Mother in private." he said pointedly, and she darted out of the room.

She went upstairs and laid on her bed, staring into space. This was a bitter blow. It had caused trouble with her Father and she would have to wait until Tuesday to know what the school had to say. It was now only Saturday morning.

Trudi thought back to the previous evening, when she and Marcus had been laughing heartily. They were laughing because they thought they were winning the battle to save the railway. It didn't look like that now. It was such a lovely steam railway and she knew there were very good reasons for saving it. She wasn't going to give up the campaign yet.

Her Father put his head around her bedroom door.

"I'm going to Mrs Redlands' house to have a chat with her. She's as concerned as I am. Your grandmother will be round in a few minutes. In the meantime, don't slip out of the house or try to contact anybody or you'll have me to answer to."

Mr Barnes slammed the back door as he left.

Gran arrived a few minutes later, looking very serious.

"He knows." she said.

"Don't worry, Gran, I didn't tell him that you knew, though I think he guessed." Trudi hugged her grandmother tightly. She seemed like her only friend in the world at the moment - at least, she would be by the time her Father had finished.

"I had a nasty feeling he would find out," said Gran.

"I know you did, Gran. I should have listened to you."

"What's happening? I understand your Father had a letter this morning."

It was still lying on the table, so Trudi showed it to her grandmother, who read it carefully.

"Your Headmistress is obviously quite upset about you using the name of the school."

"Yes, she is."

"Can you promise her that you won't take any further part in the campaign?"

"No."

"So what can you promise her?"

"I'll try - we'll try - to keep the school's name out of it."

"She's saying that you can't do that - that your campaign is now associated with the name of the school."

"I disagree."

"She's the Headmistress."

There seemed to be no answer to that. There might not be on Tuesday either.

"How's the campaign going?" Gran asked.

"We've had good coverage in the local newspaper. It's upset the man in charge of the railways but unfortunately, it's upset the school as well. The item on the local news programme was good, according to Marcus. However, the man in charge of the railways was a nasty piece of work and I don't think we've made friends with the local MP either."

Gran chuckled, "What you mean is, you've got everybody's backs up?"

"I suppose so, yes."

"So, where do you go from here?"

"Start making friends again?" Trudi laughed for the first time that morning. Then she looked more serious, "I think we're just going to have to let it take its course and see what happens."

"You won't let yourself be thrown out of Royds Well, will you?"

"I don't want to leave it."

"That's not what I asked."

"I know."

Trudi wished she could have spoken to Marcus about all of this. It had been such a shock.

Her Father returned home around lunchtime. He announced that he had had a good chat with Marcus' Mother and that she was a 'very sensible woman'.

Trudi was pleased that the two parents had not argued, though she suspected that what was said might have made her ears burn.

She and her Father hardly spoke for the rest of the day and she was pleased that Gran was in the house.

That night, as she was about to settle down in bed, her Father came to speak to her.

"You'll have to eat a lot of humble pie on Tuesday," he said. "You'd better think about how you're going to talk yourself out of being expelled."

"That won't happen, Dad."

"You're quite sure about that? You'll promise to drop this business with the railway?"

She was silent and it annoyed him.

"You and my Mother are all I've got," he said gently, before adding, "But if you get yourself thrown out of Royds Well, we're going to fall out Trudi. Big time."

With that, he departed.

Trudi lay awake for a few minutes, thinking.

The phrase 'you can't make an omelette without breaking eggs' came into her mind.

Trudi was determined to make the omelette - to save the railway; but she wasn't looking forward to breaking the eggs...

Chapter 11

A Few Minutes with the Headmistress

Tuesday morning arrived at last.

Trudi's feelings were a mixture of worry and relief that the waiting was over. By the end of today she would know what the Headmistress had to say to her - she would know indeed, whether she would be allowed to return to Royds Well High.

It had been arranged that Mrs Redlands would be collecting Trudi and her Father at a quarter past nine and they would be travelling to the school in her car.

Trudi and her Father had spoken little since Saturday morning, when Mrs Hampshire's letter had arrived. After getting over the shock of receiving the letter, Mr Barnes had been amazed that Trudi could have got herself into such trouble.

Could this be the same girl who had always got such glowing reports from her teachers? Could this be the same girl who had always been so well mannered and polite?

Even worse than the fact that Trudi had offended the School was the fact that she did not seem willing to back down. It seemed as if she would rather be expelled than give up her campaign to save the railway.

Mr Barnes had spoken of these things to Mrs Redlands more in sorrow than in anger. She had laughed.

"You think you've got problems," she had replied. "Marcus never gets glowing reports like that and he's just so lazy. I've often had to ask him two or three times, if I want him to do something."

"No," she had continued, "you don't need to worry about Trudi, Mr Barnes. I'm very glad that my son has got to know her, she'll be a good influence on him. She's a fine young woman."

"Do you think they'll push it to the limit?" Trudi's Father had asked. "Do you think they could be thrown out?"

"No," Mrs Redlands had replied. "They're not stupid."

That conversation had taken place the previous Saturday morning. As he thought back over it now, Mr Barnes hoped that Marcus' Mother was right. He was not convinced of it…

Mrs Redlands arrived a few minutes early and the adults sat in the front as they drove to Royds Well. The adults occasionally spoke during the journey, but not about the purpose of their visit. Marcus and Trudi exchanged occasional sympathetic glances. Both felt that they were under a cloud that morning and had been so for the last few days.

Riding down the drive to the front of the school, just as the teachers did every morning in their cars, seemed strange. Their parents might be treated as honoured guests at the school, but Trudi and Marcus were well aware that they wouldn't be. Indeed, they did not quite know what was in store for them.

Mrs Hampshire must have seen the car arriving and she came to greet the parents on the steps of the front entrance.

"Ah, Mrs Redlands and Mr Barnes, so good of you to come," she said, ignoring the two pupils who were with them. "Follow me," she said, leading the party to her office. "If you'd like to take a seat," she addressed the parents, "I'll take Trudi and Marcus somewhere where they'll be out of mischief. I'll be back shortly."

The pupils followed the Headmistress to the small Governors' Meeting Room, where they sat down in comfortable chairs.

"I shall be speaking to you both later," said the Headmistress coolly. "If you need to leave the room for any reason, my Secretary is next door."

She closed the door behind her; Marcus and Trudi listened to the sound of her footsteps returning to her study.

"What do you suppose they're talking about?" asked Marcus.

"Our punishment, no doubt, and whether or not we'll be allowed to return to school."

"You don't seriously think they'll throw us out?"

"My Dad does - especially if we don't agree to give up our campaign."

"Surely we can keep the school out of it from now on?"

"He says the school is bound to get dragged in if we carry on."

"I suppose we were a bit daft, putting the name of the school on our banners and saying we thought the other kids would support us. But the journalist suggested putting the school name on the banners and he asked the question about the other kids."

Sitting here, knowing that before very long the two schoolfriends would have to explain themselves, Trudi was beginning to have doubts.

"Should we just forget about the railway, Marcus?"

"No way." Marcus pictured the steam train he had so enjoyed riding on. "We mustn't give it up, unless we're forced to promise we will, in order to return to school. We must try to avoid promising anything, but if we carry on the campaign, we'll have to keep the school's name out of it."

"So we stay in school at all costs?"

"We've not got much choice, Trudi."

"My Father will be pleased."

A few minutes later Mrs Hampshire came back into the room, followed by the two parents.

"I shall be with you two in a moment," said the Headmistress. "Mrs Redlands and Mr Barnes, I'll just take you along to my Deputy, she'll look after you."

Marcus and Trudi looked at their parents, whose faces gave nothing away.

"I see they're not hanging around to witness the trial and verdict, then." Marcus muttered, only half joking, when the two pupils were alone again.

Trudi glanced at him and answered with a smile.

"Right, follow me." barked the Headmistress, putting her head around the door. The children walked behind her to her study.

Mrs Hampshire sat down on a large chair behind her desk. The two friends were about to sit down on the chairs in front of the desk.

"I'm not going to ask you to sit down." said the Headmistress coldly. The pupils immediately stood up again as if they had just sat on an electric cable.

"You two have caused me a great deal of embarrassment. I have written to the railway company to make it clear that this school does not have any opinions about the closure of the railway line, and I have written to the local newspaper to say the same thing. Do you know that my telephone hardly stopped ringing yesterday morning, with people wanting to express this or that opinion about the closure of the railway line? Fortunately I was out, but my secretary was wasting all her time talking to people about the railway. She wasn't able to get on with her work."

"We're sorry, Miss." chorused Marcus and Trudi together.

"I'm afraid that 'sorry' is not quite good enough. I might tell you that the local council is also very upset that this school is seen to be involved in politics. In case you don't know, Marcus and Trudi, they're my employers and I'm not going to lose my job for your sake."

There was silence for a moment before she continued, "I'm told that Mr Holland, the man who did this job before I did, was very strict and he ran this school through fear."

She paused again. "I arrived here eight years ago as last September - you would have been four then - and I promised myself that I wasn't going to be like that. Plenty of older teachers and over half of the Governors think that pupils were better behaved when Mr Holland was here, and they want me to run the school in the way he did. They would like me to make an example of you. Those teachers and Governors do not run this school," - the pupils looked visibly relieved - "but nor, Trudi and Marcus, do you."

She looked Trudi straight in the eye. "I understand young lady, that you are not willing to promise your father that you will cease to be involved in the campaign to save the railway?"

No answer was invited. The Headmistress paused, studying Marcus as well.

"I'm not going to ask either of you to make me a promise but I'm going to give you one. If you carry on with your campaign, and the newspapers and television continue to associate this school with it, you will both be expelled. Do you understand?"

"Yes, Miss." chorused both pupils glumly.

"Good," said Mrs Hampshire. "We all know where we stand, then. Your parents know about that condition and I wanted to give you some time to think it over, so you won't be returning to school until Friday morning. You must decide in the meantime whether you really want to stay here. Do either of you have any questions?"

They didn't. They had been given a clear choice, and it looked as if the campaign would have to stop.

"I'm going to take you back to the Governors' Meeting Room for a few minutes until your parents are ready to collect you. If you think of any questions during that time, please knock on my door."

"Game, set and match to Mrs Hampshire," said Trudi when they were once again on their own. "I've got to admit - she handled that brilliantly."

"Yes," agreed Marcus. "She didn't punish us; she didn't ask us to make any promises we might have felt uncomfortable making but she made it clear we could be expelled if we didn't pull out of the campaign."

"So what do we do now?"

"We can't use the newspaper again, that's for certain. I suppose we don't need to now, hopefully people will have heard about the line closure. I don't see why we can't write to people though."

"Like who?"

"The local MP, for instance?"

"He's useless!" exclaimed Trudi. "Still, if we can do anything at all, it's better than doing nothing."

Footsteps could now be heard approaching and the two friends fell silent. The door opened and Mrs Hampshire walked in, followed by the parents.

Turning to the adults, Mrs Hampshire said, "I've explained what we agreed to Marcus and Trudi. I hope we can put this behind us now."

She then directed her conversation to the friends and spoke rather more kindly than she had done earlier. "I'm looking forward to seeing you back at school on Friday. I'm sure none of us will have any hard feelings."

The journey back home was much like the journey to school had been, very little was said.

Trudi lay down on her bed when she got home. So now she knew. She wouldn't be leaving school and the railway *might* or *might not* be saved.

She and Marcus would have very little to do with that and they certainly wouldn't get the credit for it.

The dream, it seemed, was over...

Chapter 12

'Prison'

Any hopes Trudi might have had that she would spend part of the next couple of days with Marcus were soon dashed.

That evening her Father said, "The Headmistress was very anxious that you and Marcus should have the chance to think about what you have done, and how you are going to behave in the future, before you go back to school."

Trudi waited. She had a good idea what her Father was going to say and she was right.

"She also thought it would be wrong if you and Marcus were enjoying yourselves while the other pupils are at school. I am at work, tomorrow, as you know. So is Marcus' Mother. Your Grandmother will be here, and she is under strict instructions not to allow you to leave the house on your own, and not to allow you to use the telephone."

"Dad!" exclaimed Trudi.

"I'm not arguing, young lady. You and Marcus have caused a lot of trouble to a lot of people. Mrs Hampshire has been receiving telephone calls about the railway, which is nothing to do with her, when she has a school to run. She's also been in bother with the Council about it. Mrs Redlands and I have both taken a day off work today to go to the school. No, Trudi," he concluded. "You should be thankful you have got off so lightly."

Trudi knew that it would be useless to argue any further and, in any case, perhaps her Father was right. Things could have been more serious.

"You will see Marcus again on Friday morning." said Mr Barnes kindly, noticing his daughter's gloomy face.

Trudi found the following morning very frustrating. She couldn't go to school, of course, but she could read, play games with her grandmother and go out with the older lady. She enjoyed all of these things, but she liked to be able to get out on her own too.

It was lunchtime when she was suddenly struck with horror. The letter she and Marcus had written to the local newspaper the previous week, unless stopped would be published in the *Recorder* on Friday and there would be more bother at school. Rushing upstairs after lunch, Trudi scribbled a note to Marcus, asking him to contact the newspaper to stop publication of the letter.

She thought it unlikely that her grandmother would allow her to visit or telephone the newspaper office.

"Gran," she said, going downstairs again. "Do you mind if I slip to Marcus' house to deliver a note…"

"Sorry, dear."

"It's very urgent. You can come with me if you want. I promise I won't speak to him…"

"No, dear."

"Can I telephone him then?"

"No, dear. I gave a promise to your Father and I'm going to keep it."

Trudi helped her grandmother with the washing up and then went upstairs to her Father's bedroom. Her own looked out on to the back garden but his looked out on to the street. It seemed as if this was the closest, she was going to get to the outside world that day…

As she stared out of the window, Trudi wondered if she ought to tell Gran about the problem. She would surely let her deliver the letter then. In the distance she noticed a blonde-haired figure, holding a dog on a lead and carrying an orange-coloured bag over her shoulder, walking along the street towards her. She thought it couldn't be, but it was, Jane the paper girl who was about fifteen. They had often chatted during the school holidays; Trudi quickly wrote Marcus' address on the envelope of the note. She opened the bedroom window.

"Jane," she called down as if the girl had been her oldest friend. "Do you deliver to...?" She quoted Marcus' address.

"I don't deliver to that house, but I go down that road." replied the girl.

"Could you deliver this for me?" Trudi asked, holding the letter out of the window.

"Course I can. I'll be there in ten minutes."

"Thanks." Trudi dropped the letter, which Jane managed to catch. "Why are you off school, Jane?" she asked curiously.

"It's our half-term holiday, it's later than yours. I thought you would have been back."

"I should have been," replied Trudi. "It's a long story. By the way, here's two shillings for your trouble." She dropped the coin.

"Don't be silly, Trudi. I don't need two shillings for sticking a note through somebody's door. I'll put it back through your letterbox."

"Thanks, Jane. Could you ring his doorbell when you deliver it, so he knows it's there?"

Jane grinned. "Will do. You don't want me to polish his doorstep while I'm about it?"

Trudi laughed. "Now you come to mention it..."

"I should have kept that two shillings," said Jane with a twinkle in her eye. "Anyway, I'd better be going before you give me any more jobs, and before this dog pulls me over. He's getting very impatient."

"Thanks! See you, Jane." Trudi watched as the girl disappeared.

She went downstairs to pick up the two-shilling coin.

"I've just seen a coin on the mat by the letterbox, Trudi. Did you drop it there?" asked Gran.

"No." The girl was determined not to lie - and especially not to her grandmother.

"It must be mine, then," replied Gran. "I swept the hall this morning and it wasn't there then."

Trudi watched as her grandmother put the money in her purse. She could hardly explain why the coin had been there. Later that afternoon, Gran made some cocoa and got out a delicious cake she had bought that morning and she and Trudi sat down to afternoon tea.

"You've been very good, today," said Gran. "I know you don't like being stuck in the house but you didn't argue when I said you couldn't go out." The older lady opened her purse. "I'm giving you two shillings for making today much more pleasant than I expected it to be."

"Thank you, Gran."

"Of course," added her grandmother, smiling. "You might have dropped that two shillings on the doormat today - it might not have been mine at all so just in case, I'll give you another."

Trudi's eyes shone. Could Gran have overheard the conversation with the newspaper girl and known where the coin had come from all along? The more she thought about it, the surer she was. Good old Gran...

Ten minutes later, at about twenty to three, Marcus' doorbell rang. The newspaper girl grinned when he opened the door. "I presume you're Marcus. Special delivery from Trudi."

"Thanks," he replied. "What's your name?"

"Jane. Trudi said it was urgent." The newspaper girl was about to go, but curiosity got the better of her.

"Why aren't you at school?"

Marcus blushed. "We're... in bother." he said. "We started a campaign to save the Banham railway line and we got into trouble for using the name of the school. 'The Recorder' printed a piece and our Headmistress didn't like it."

"That's why Trudi's at home, too?"

"Yes."

"There's a piece about the railway in the evening paper. You don't get one, do you?"

"How do you know what's in the evening paper?" asked Marcus, good-humouredly. "You're supposed to deliver them, not read them."

"Well, if I feel tired in the middle of my round, I sometimes sit down on a wall and…"

"Read somebody else's paper?" he said triumphantly.

"If that's what you think, I'm certainly not going to show you somebody else's paper." she teased, waving a folded newspaper in front of him.

"All right, you win."

"Front page, right-hand side." Jane unfolded the newspaper so that Marcus could read it.

COUNCILLORS PROTEST AT RAIL CLOSURE

'Councillors on Royds Well District Council, including those representing the Banham area, agreed yesterday to write to the railway company to protest at the intended closure of the Royds Well to Banham Branch line.

Their letter will point out that many people in Banham do not have cars and prefer to ride on a train rather than a bus. Councillors will also argue that the steam train service, one of very few now running on the railways, could be promoted as a tourist attraction.'

Marcus returned the newspaper to the girl, who folded it ready to put in his neighbour's letterbox.

"Thanks, Jane. I've hardly spoken to anyone over the last few days. I've really enjoyed our chat."

"Get away with you," she laughed, hitting him on the head with the newspaper in fun. "I'd better deliver some more papers before I get into bother."

After Jane had gone on her way, Marcus opened the note.

Of course, that wretched letter they had sent to the newspaper - Marcus would have to stop them printing it. Otherwise, he and Trudi might be trailing into school with their parents next week too...

He checked the number of the '*Banham Recorder*' and dialled it.

"Mark Richards, please." he said, as the phone was answered, and soon he was put through. "Sorry to bother you," said Marcus to the journalist. "I was involved in the demonstration to save the railway - do you remember?"

"Of course I remember, Marcus. How can I help?"

"We gave you a letter for the newspaper last Friday. Is there any chance you can stop them publishing it?"

The journalist hesitated. "I can try," he said. "It's only Wednesday afternoon - yes, I'll see what I can do. I'll have to speak to the Royds Well Office, you know, that's where they print it."

Mr Richards paused again, then said, "I don't know why you don't want it published. It was a brilliant letter."

"We got into trouble at school for it." replied Marcus. "They didn't like us using the name of the school on the banners and when we spoke to you."

"That's a shame."

"Mrs Hampshire - the Headmistress, you know, has told us we will be expelled if we get the school's name in the paper again in connection with this."

"Really? How awful! Has she imposed any other punishment on you?"

"No, just that. You see how important it is that you don't publish that letter?"

"Of course. I'll slip across to Royds Well and sort it out myself this afternoon. Leave it with me."

"Thanks, Mr Richards."

"Don't mention it."

Relieved, Marcus put the telephone down.

The journalist spent a few minutes at his typewriter before dashing out of the office to his car. He had to catch the Royds Well office as soon as possible.

"So what mischief have you been up to today, then?" Marcus' Mother seemed in a good mood when she returned home from work.

"Mischief? Me?" he grinned.

"It's not exactly unheard of, Marcus." His Mother ruffled his hair playfully.

"Mum." This was as good a time as any to ask. "Could I slip out this evening to see Trudi?"

His Mother looked serious. "Her Father and I agreed that you wouldn't see one another until Friday."

Mrs Redlands thought for a moment.

"You may go for a walk if you wish. If that walk takes you to Trudi's house - well, you'll have to see what her Father says. Just don't be surprised if he says 'no'."

"Thanks, Mum." Marcus gave her a hug.

"Now, what you can do for me Marcus, is to wash that big pile of dishes over there…"

So it was that a little after seven o'clock, Marcus left the house. Although there had been nobody to check on him, he had followed his Mother's instructions to stay in during the daytime. Now he was glad of the fresh air. Above all, though, he was looking forward to speaking to Trudi again…

Chapter 13

Escape

'She searched the room looking for possible ways of escape but could find none. The door was locked, and the key had not been left in it. The fireplace had been filled in and there were bars over the windows.

"It's no good," she thought. "I'm trapped. I'll just have to wait until they come back to set me free or take me somewhere else with them. If only I could get out…'

There was the sound of gravel on the window.

'I say,' thought Trudi. '*Emma's Adventures* are so realistic. That might almost have been my bedroom window.' The sound came again. Trudi glanced at the page once more. No, there was no reference to somebody throwing gravel at a window there. Could it really have been outside?

Trudi looked out of her bedroom window and was surprised to see Marcus in the garden.

She signalled to him to wait a moment. Very quickly, she changed out of the skirt she was wearing into a pair of jeans.

Going back to the window, she opened it and felt the branch of a tree which was just outside. Yes, she was sure that it could bear her weight.

Signalling to Marcus to keep silent, she climbed out of the window, edged along the branch then climbed down the very thick trunk of the tree.

"Follow me," she whispered. Her heart was pounding madly - this could go horribly wrong.

The only window down the side of the house was half-way up the stairs, so the two friends needed only to lower their heads to make sure they were not seen.

Trudi got down on her hands and knees in order to go past the front of the house and Marcus followed suit. They continued to crawl until Trudi was sure they couldn't be seen from the house. Marcus' knees felt quite sore by the time they stood up again.

"You didn't tell me that you did a Tarzan act," he said, still amazed at the way Trudi had climbed out of the house. "Do you do that often?"

She laughed. "I've never done it before. I'm not sure I should have done it either - my hands and knees are quite sore."

"You're not the only one."

"What did you want to say to me?"

"Just to say 'hello', really. I didn't expect you to go to all this trouble."

"How are things?" asked Trudi.

"Not too bad. Mum told me to stay in today, so I did. I got your note, though."

"You rang Mark Richards?"

"Yes."

"Can he stop them publishing the letter?" Trudi asked.

"I hope so. I told him we were for the high jump if he couldn't."

"That's one less worry for us, then."

The two schoolfriends walked towards the park in Banham. "How are things with you?" asked Marcus.

"Dad's not happy," replied Trudi solemnly. Then she grinned. "That's the trouble with getting good reports, Marcus. People expect great things of you."

He laughed, "I wouldn't know."

Trudi continued earnestly, "Dad doesn't like it at all Marcus. I suppose it's the first time his 'little girl' has got herself into bother."

"I must admit, Trudi, when I sat opposite you on the train just before half term, I decided that you had never been in trouble in your life and probably never would be. I thought I'd like you better if you occasionally did something wrong."

"We must have become the best of friends over the last few days then Marcus," she joked.

There was silence for a moment or so as the two walked into the green park with its delightful pond.

"I've had arguments with Dad like anybody else does," added Trudi. "He's told me off from time to time, probably for very good reason. But we've always been very close, especially since Mum died. The last few days have been different. I've been glad that my grandmother has been around or it would have been unbearable. Dad and I have hardly spoken."

"Do you see much of your grandmother?"

"Quite a lot. She lives near and she usually spends the day with me during school holidays. During the term, she usually has tea at our house so she's there when I get home. Dad gets in later. You'd like her, Marcus."

"I like your Father, too, though I wasn't very pleased when he told me I couldn't speak to you. Why's he so upset?" Marcus asked, frowning.

"I suppose it's because we have been so close and I couldn't tell him about the railway. Perhaps he feels it's as if I lied to him and I suppose I almost did."

"Almost?"

"I hid the front page of the local newspaper and replaced it with the front page of the previous week's, so that he wouldn't read about the demonstration.

I got Gran to have a private chat with him while the regional news was on television, so that he didn't see us on that. Gran warned me that I couldn't keep it from him for long - I should have listened..."

"Naughty girl!" exclaimed Marcus, "I hope he doesn't think I'm a bad influence."

"You are, aren't you?"

Marcus gave her a friendly punch.

They sat down on a wooden bench, gazing at the pond as the light faded.

"I'm not proud of myself, you know, Marcus." Trudi was still in a gloomy mood. "I should have spoken to him about the railway before Mrs Hampshire wrote."

"Would he have let you get involved?"

"I don't know, but some things are even more important than steam railways."

Marcus said nothing.

Trudi stood up. "I just hope he doesn't find out about tonight's adventure."

"What would he do?" asked Marcus, worried.

"Just send a few sharp words in my direction. Don't worry, Marcus. He was watching a film on television which doesn't finish until ten o'clock, so he'll be glued to that. He won't know a thing."

She smiled. "Sorry if I've been poor company this evening. Race you round the pond and then we'd better go home."

Marcus was startled but quickly set off running. He was surprised to come second.

"Are you looking forward to going back to school on Friday?" asked Trudi.

Marcus laughed: "I never thought I would miss it, but the last day or so has been rather boring."

"I shall be glad, too," said Trudi. "Life will seem more - normal."

"Yes, I wonder how much our schoolfriends know about our involvement with the railway and the trouble it has brought us."

"I bet most of them have seen our pictures in the local paper last weekend, since it was in the Royds Well edition as well. I hope they don't know we've been told to stay off school for a few days."

"Still the same old Trudi, anxious not to get into bother."

She said nothing and Marcus looked at her again. His opinion of her had changed a lot since he had first seen her as a stuck-up girl who spent her time with her nose in her schoolbooks when she was not trying to please the adults around her. Trudi was a good and loyal companion, he decided, and she had stuck her neck out over the railway.

He could never have imagined the girl he had known so little about even two weeks ago climbing out of her bedroom window and shinning down a tree.

Miss Loxley and Mrs Hampshire too, would probably never see her in the same way again.

Marcus wondered - a little sadly - whether he would ever again see the Trudi he had seen for the last ten days. He certainly had the impression that she felt she had offended too many people. They walked back to Trudi's house, both deep in thought. As they turned to walk up her road, Trudi broke the silence:

"I'm really glad that you called, Marcus. I've enjoyed this evening. It's been good to have someone to talk to."

"I've enjoyed it too. I'll follow you into your back garden and make sure you get into the house safely."

Trudi glanced up the road towards her house. The curtains were now drawn in the sitting room, so there was no need to crawl on the ground again. The light was on. Good. Her Father was still watching the film then. It was not quite nine o'clock.

The two friends walked up the drive as quietly as possible, ducking as they went past the window at the side and standing up again when they were in the back garden.

Trudi studied the tree and the branch which was close to her room. Could she get back that way? Yes, she thought she could.

"See you on Friday." whispered Marcus.

He watched as she climbed the tree then edged herself along the branch towards the window, which was still open. She eased her feet on to the ledge. Catching hold of the top of the window, she turned herself round slightly before climbing back into the room. The light was no longer on in her room. Had she switched it off when she went out? She couldn't remember. She hoped this did not mean her Father had discovered her absence.

She turned on the light and lay down on her bed, intending to read more of 'Emma's Adventures.'

There was a knock on the door.

"You're back, I see," said her Father, putting his head round the door.

"How did you know I was out?" Trudi had not expected this.

"I came up to speak to you during one of the advert breaks in the film."

"Marcus called."

"I know. I told him you couldn't speak to him this evening."

"He - walked round the back of the house..."

"... and suggested you climb out of the window, I suppose?"

"That was my idea."

"Really?"

"I'm not lying, Dad. Marcus just wanted to talk to me."

"Where did you go?"

"The park. We just sat and chatted and then had a race around the pond." Trudi could feel her heart beating madly.

"If I telephoned Marcus, would he confirm your story?"

"Yes, but please don't. He'd probably get into trouble."

"I'm not going to, Trudi. I believe you."

Mr Barnes sighed heavily and there was silence. Then he said, "Trudi, I do believe what you've told me, but I feel I can't trust you anymore. I told you that you weren't allowed to talk to Marcus or go out with him until Friday, and you have gone against my wishes. We really are going to fall out big time if you carry on like this."

He paused again, before saying, "Good Night, Trudi." That probably wasn't an instruction to go to bed, but Trudi decided to do so anyway. It had seemed like a long day and tomorrow would be the same. Once in bed, she lay awake for a long time.

Trudi and her Father had always been close – "as thick as thieves," an aunt had once said – both before and especially after her Mother died.

Now they were drifting apart. Trudi would give up almost anything or anyone to save that relationship – and that included Marcus, if she had to.

Chapter 14

More Fireworks

"Trudi Barnes, Marcus Redlands - my Office NOW!"

Friday morning had started so well. Trudi's Father had gently urged her to stay out of trouble and she had given him a hug. She did not expect that they would be fighting any more. Meanwhile, Marcus' Mother had good-humouredly told him to keep out of mischief. Marcus and Trudi had sat together on the train to Royds Well - it had been good to be able to talk without being secretive.

When they got to school, they had a private chat with their form-mistress, Miss Loxley. She said that other pupils in the class had not been told why they had been away from school and would therefore assume that they had been ill. They should now settle down and get on with their work.

So everything seemed to be back to normal - until the Headmistress arrived beetroot-faced, to call the two schoolfriends out of their English lesson.

Shocked and wondering whatever could have gone wrong, the two friends followed Mrs Hampshire as she marched through the corridors to her office. Marcus took Trudi's hand and squeezed it as they walked along. They were in this together.

The Headmistress almost slammed the door of her study behind them. The two friends stood in front of her desk, neither conscious that Marcus was still holding Trudi's hand.

"I think you can stop holding hands now." said Mrs Hampshire, irritated. She glanced at the pale faces across the desk from her, "You'd better sit down."

Remembering that she had made them stand the previous occasion, Trudi and Marcus were not sure whether this was good news or bad news. As the Headmistress' face still looked like thunder, they suspected it was bad news.

"Perhaps," said Mrs Hampshire quietly, "you would like to explain this."

She passed a copy of the '*Royds Well Recorder*' across the desk. The friends gazed at the front page with horror.

"You might as well read the story as well," said the Headmistress coldly. "You feature prominently in the newspaper and I've got all day."

So, very uncomfortably, Marcus and Trudi read the piece...

RAILWAY CAMPAIGN PUPILS FACE EXPULSION

Royds Well High cracks down on free speech.

Royds Well High School pupils Trudi Barnes and Marcus Redlands have been warned that they may be expelled – for putting the school's name on a banner and writing a letter to this newspaper. As we reported last week, the two friends organised a demonstration against the proposed closure on March 31st next year of the Royds Well to Banham branch railway line. The two twelve-year old pupils, who use the line to get to school, carried banners with the words:

'Royds Well High Pupils say No to Rail Closure'

———

At the time, Marcus Redlands told us: The pupils of Royds Well High School agree with us. Headmistress Jennifer Hampshire, who clearly thinks that children should neither be seen nor heard, has told the pupils that they must give up the campaign – or leave the school.

To read the letter the Headmistress did not wish you to see, turn to page eight. See also our editorial comment on the same page...

Marcus and Trudi turned to page eight. They read their own letter first. Seeing the letter in print, Marcus and Trudi were still proud of their handiwork. The heading above it, was however, unfortunate.

THE ROYDS WELL REBELS - WHAT THEY WROTE...

Dear Sir

We have started a campaign to save the railway line from Royds Well to Banham and we would like to explain some of the reasons for it to your readers.

More and more people are using cars, vans and lorries on the roads and this seems to be the reason why the railway company wants to close the line. However, we believe that one day, if the growth of traffic continues, the roads will be so blocked up that people will want to use trains again. If the trains stop running now, the track will no doubt be taken up – so people won't have that

choice in future years.

It is argued that there is also a bus service between Royds Well and Banham. So there is, but a train can carry more people. Surely the bus company and the railway company can work together so that they are not fighting over the same passengers? We urge your readers to support our campaign but also to use this railway line whenever they can.

Yours Faithfully
Marcus Redlands
Trudi Barnes
Royds Well High School

FREE SPEECH

You will no doubt have read the letter from twelve-year old pupils Marcus Redlands and Trudi Barnes. They argue passionately for saving the railway line from Royds Well to Banham and they set out a very good case. You might agree or disagree with them.

It is very unlikely that you will think that they should be expelled from school for writing it - unless that is, you are Jennifer Hampshire, their Headmistress. As our reporter said in the article on the front page, she seems to think that children should neither be seen nor heard.

We disagree! It is now 1966, not 1866. Adults in our country enjoy free speech and children should, too.

As it happens, we support this campaign and we wish Trudi and Marcus every success with it. Even if we didn't, we would say to Jennifer Hampshire and Royds Well High School: 'Celebrate this contribution by future voters and citizens of our country and do not deny them the right to express their opinions.'

The friends turned back to the front page of the newspaper. The article was complete, with a reprint of the photograph of the demonstration from the previous week, and pictures of the two pupils somewhat larger than those which the newspaper had published in its last edition.

The '*Royds Well Recorder*' - and no doubt its '*Banham Recorder*' edition too, had reopened old wounds. Marcus and Trudi were now in as much trouble as they had been the previous Saturday, when Mrs Hampshire's letters to their parents had arrived.

"I'm sorry." said Trudi, hardly daring to look at the Headmistress.

"You're sorry." The woman moved around her desk and was almost standing over the two pupils now. "YOU'RE SORRY. How do you think I feel? Being presented in the local newspaper almost as a wicked witch?"

"Not very good, Miss." replied Trudi as the Headmistress glared at her.

"*Not very good, Miss* - that's right. Perhaps you would like to tell me how the local newspaper found out about our private conversation - I certainly didn't tell them."

"I did, Mrs Hampshire." said Marcus, meekly.

"I see. You thought you would get some sympathy from the newspaper, did you?"

"It wasn't like that."

"Then perhaps you will tell me how it was?"

"We - Trudi and I - wrote that letter and handed it in at the newspaper office last Friday. The local reporter Mark Richards said it would be a good way of getting publicity for the railway. Then our parents got your letters on Saturday and it was such a shock to us that we forgot all about the letter to the newspaper."

"Until Wednesday," prompted Trudi.

"Trudi suddenly remembered on Wednesday so she sent me a note - our parents weren't allowing us to see or talk to one another."

"Sent you a note? How?" asked the Headmistress.

"The newspaper girl delivered it." replied Trudi.

"I see." Mrs Hampshire turned to Marcus. "So what did you do?"

"I phoned the Banham office of *The Recorder* and asked them not to publish our letter."

"You obviously gave reasons?"

"Yes, Miss."

"The reporter you spoke to was Mark Richards?"

"Yes, Miss."

"You had dealt with him before?"

"Yes, Miss. We told him about the demonstration, and he agreed to put a poster in the window of the newspaper office. He also wrote the report in last week's paper. He was very sympathetic."

The Headmistress snorted. "Very sympathetic? Has it not occurred to you Marcus, how incredibly stupid you two have been? There's a young ambitious reporter sitting in his office at Banham wondering how he can get his stories into the main edition of *The Recorder* – *'The Royds Well Recorder'*. Then you go along with your campaign to save the railway and he sees his opportunity. Did he by any chance encourage you to put the name of the school on your banners and the letter?"

Marcus and Trudi grimaced. "Yes, he did."

"You've been set up!" exclaimed Mrs Hampshire. "Your reporter friend has used you to get his story on the front page of the paper. That's all he's interested in, not the railway."

The Headmistress was silent for a moment, before adding, "Half of the Governors and several of the older teachers have been baying for your blood already this morning. You're a couple of idiots and you've done a lot of damage to the school. I am particularly concerned that the article says I have tried to stop your campaign when I told you that you should make sure the school's name was not linked to it. I have written a letter to the newspaper and they will no doubt correct it - a week late. I wouldn't be surprised if I had a few nasty telephone calls in the meantime and I shall blame you for them."

Mrs Hampshire glanced at the two pupils, who were now sitting very shame-faced.

"There remains the question of your fate. My first thought was to send you both straight home, but I have decided to let you stay here for the rest of the day. I'm not going to ask the Governors to throw you out, but the council might. After reading that vicious article, I shall have to consider very seriously whether I wish to defend you."

"You mean we might be expelled?" Trudi looked almost tearful.

"You were warned. Perhaps it's as well for all of us that tomorrow is Saturday. Everybody might have cooled off by Monday."

She glanced at her watch. "You've missed your English lesson and your class will be in the middle of the Geography lesson now. I don't see why you should interrupt them - you can go to your next lesson when it starts in half an hour. In the meantime I suggest you go for a walk in the school grounds and get some fresh air. Now get out of my sight."

Neither Marcus nor Trudi needed to be asked twice...

Chapter 15

A Glimmer of Hope

"Trudi and Marcus, Mrs Hampshire would like to have another word with you."

The rest of the day had passed smoothly enough, and the two friends could not imagine why the Headmistress would suddenly want to see them now, towards the end of the afternoon. Nothing else could possibly have gone wrong - surely?

"Listen you two," said Miss Loxley, noticing their worried faces. "I know you are trying to save the railway line and you have had a few problems. There is someone who might be able to help you."

"You?" asked Marcus surprised.

Miss Loxley laughed. "No, not me. My Father, Brian Loxley knows the Chairman of Governors here, Mike Stephens very well. Mr Stephens runs MS Engineering in Royds Well. He's a millionaire and he's very interested in railways."

The others hardly dared to interrupt.

"If you need somebody to help your campaign, Mike Stephens might just be your man."

Trudi and Marcus were amazed. They had tried to keep their plans to save the railway a secret and if they had but opened their mouths the answer was - or at least might be - in their own classroom.

Miss Loxley suddenly looked anxious, "I'm telling you this because I want to help. I trust you not to repeat it," she said.

The others nodded: "We won't say anything."

"Alright. Tomorrow is Saturday. I suggest you both go into Royds Well in the morning and ask to speak to Mike Stephens at the Firm - I'll give you the address. Tell him Jill Loxley sent you."

Then she added, looking earnest, "and if you ever - EVER - repeat my first name on the school premises, I'll put you both in detention until the end of term."

Trudi wondered whether this gentle woman would ever carry out such a threat. "Don't worry," she said. "We'll keep your secret."

"I'm sure you will," replied her form-mistress. "Now you two run along to see Mrs Hampshire and tell her I held you up if she complains you're late."

"Miss Loxley is lovely, isn't she?" said Trudi as they were making their way along the now familiar corridors to the Headmistress' study.

"Yes, I like her too," agreed Marcus.

He knocked on the door of the office a little apprehensively.

"Come in!" shouted a voice from inside. It was Mrs Hampshire's.

"Sit down, please," she said as the pupils entered, "and shut the door behind you."

They sat down, feeling that they had seen this room a little too often recently.

"I had a telephone call this afternoon from a Mr Belstone," began the Headmistress. "He's the Regional Director of the railway company. He tells me that you two and another boy, arranged to see him by telling him that you hoped to buy the line."

"That's not true," Marcus called out before he could stop himself.

"Then perhaps you could tell me what is true." Mrs Hampshire seemed much calmer than this morning.

"My cousin who is sixteen and sounds very grown-up, telephoned Mr Belstone and asked if we could meet him to discuss our ideas for the railway. We never suggested that we wanted to buy it."

"I believe you." replied the Headmistress.

Marcus nearly fell off his chair. "Pardon?"

"I said I believe you. I didn't like the sound of Mr Belstone - I thought he was just causing trouble." She hesitated and looked earnestly at the two pupils. "Listen, Marcus and Trudi, you must tell me now if

151

there's anybody else you have spoken to about the railway who is likely to complain about you - anybody at all."

"We've spoken to the Station Master about it," replied Trudi. "Sid Parkes - a nice old man. He's on our side - he certainly won't complain about us."

"We also spoke to the local MP, George Scott," added Marcus. "He wasn't very helpful – I don't think he'll be doing anything to save the railway, but I don't think he'll complain about us either."

"Nobody else?"

"Nobody else." replied Marcus, and Trudi nodded her head in agreement.

"Alright." The Headmistress paused. "I was very hurt - very hurt indeed - by the articles in today's local newspaper. However, I understand from what you have told me that you tried to keep the school's name out of any further publicity - and I believe you. I have therefore decided that, if any of the senior staff or the Governors ask for either of you to be expelled, I will support *you* against them. Let me give you some advice, however," The Headmistress turned to Trudi.

"You are very fortunate, Trudi, that your work at school is excellent and all your teachers speak well of you. As for you, Marcus, your teachers agree that you are a bright pupil, but one who is ready to play the fool from time to time. One day that might get you into serious bother. I suggest that you take a leaf out of Trudi's book. My advice to you both is to stay away from publicity and to stop your campaign, unless you can keep the name of the school out of it. Now, you may go." The two pupils headed hastily for the door.

"One final thing…" Marcus and Trudi glanced anxiously at the Headmistress. "I hope they don't close the railway. I am human, you know." She smiled.

Trudi's next worry was what her Father would say about her being splashed across the front page of the local newspaper. She assumed - correctly - that 'The Banham Recorder' would carry the same headline as the Royds Well edition on this occasion. She did not consider hiding the front page again. Her Father would not be fooled if she did.

Trudi was lying on her bed, reading 'Emma's Adventures', when her Father came up to speak to her.

"Have you seen the local newspaper?"

"Yes."

"Has Mrs Hampshire?"

"Yes."

What did she say?"

"That Marcus and I ought to be more careful about talking to journalists but that she would forgive us."

Mr Barnes smiled. "Then I suppose I had better do the same. We'll say no more about it."

Trudi watched in astonishment as her Father left the room. She had expected that he would have quite a lot to say about the matter.

That evening, just before going to bed, Trudi went downstairs to the sitting room to speak to her Father.

"Dad."

"Yes?"

"Will you allow me to go into Royds Well with Marcus tomorrow morning?"

"Why?"

"Miss Loxley, our form-teacher, said there was somebody there who might help us with the railway campaign."

"Your visit won't get you into the local newspaper?"

"No."

Mr Barnes looked earnest. "Let's be quite clear about this. You get yourself splashed over the front page of the local paper, upsetting your Headmistress and forcing me and Marcus' Mother to go and see her. You climb out of your bedroom window when I won't allow Marcus to see you. You get yourself splashed over the newspaper again - and you want permission to go to Royds Well tomorrow?"

"Yes," she grinned.

"Alright."

"Oh, Dad - Miss Loxley says this man can help us. Wait a minute - did you say yes?"

"I did."

Trudi was so pleased that she flung herself on her Father and gave him a hug. "I love you, Dad."

He smiled, "and I'm quite fond of you as well," he said. "Now I think it's about time you went to bed."

"Goodnight, Dad." She gave him a kiss.

"Night, Trudi. Sleep well and don't spend too long reading *Emma's Adventures*."

'Good old Dad,' she thought as she almost raced up the stairs. Things were back to normal now, and Trudi was determined that they would stay that way.

That night, Trudi dreamed that she and Marcus met Philip Belstone, the railway boss, in a remote house. He took them into a room at the top of the house and locked the door. Somehow the two schoolfriends managed to escape by climbing along the branches of a tree and shinning down it, before dashing to catch the train to Royds Well. Once there, they met Mike Stephens, a kindly man who looked to be in his eighties.

He announced that he would buy the railway for the children and wrote out the cheque in front of them. An audience had gathered and a group of people - including the Headmistress and the local MP - stood clapping Marcus and Trudi.

She woke up, feeling delighted that they had managed to save the railway, then realised that she had only been dreaming. Even so, it was a bright sunny day and she was going with Marcus to Royds Well to see Mike Stephens. They might not yet have saved the railway, but she was sure they would have done so by the end of the day. Wide awake, she flung off the bedclothes and got up.

Marcus and Trudi caught the 9:30 a.m. train to Royds Well. They were at Banham station in good time to catch this and so had time for a long chat with the station master about their adventures. Having read his copy of the local newspaper, Sid was very pleased to hear that (as far as they knew), the two friends were not about to be expelled from Royds Well High School.

The railwayman whistled with admiration after hearing the whole story. "You kids get away with a lot more than I ever could." he said.

"That's because of our charm." Trudi said, laughing.

Sid grinned. "I could believe that of you, young Miss," he said. "I wouldn't be surprised if you haven't talked yourself out of a few awkward situations before now."

Trudi blushed. This remark was a little too close to the truth for comfort!

The friends felt a little nervous as they rode on the train to Royds Well. They had never met a millionaire before, and they would have just one opportunity to persuade him to help. It seemed a great responsibility.

"What do we want him to do?" Trudi asked. It was an obvious question but not one the friends had considered.

"I suppose we want him to put pressure on the railway company to keep the line open," replied Marcus. "If not, perhaps he might buy the line himself?"

They soon found the MS Engineering works from Miss Loxley's description and presented themselves at reception.

"We'd like to see Mr Stephens," Trudi said to the young receptionist. "Could you tell him Jill Loxley asked us to call?"

The woman buzzed through on the internal telephone and then spoke to the friends.

"He'll be down in a minute," she said. "Would you like to take a seat?"

They sat down, still feeling nervous. Trudi had dreamed of an elderly man who needed no persuading of the case to save the railway. It was unlikely to be quite as easy as that...

Chapter 16

Mike Stephens

Mike Stephens bustled into reception after about five minutes. A tall, grey-haired man with a kindly face, he was perhaps around sixty years old.

"If you're friends of Jill Loxley, you'd better come upstairs," he said.

They followed him as he marched up two flights of stairs and past a noisy workshop to an office labelled "M. Stephens Managing Director." Once inside, he motioned to them to sit down in two comfortable chairs on one side of the desk, while he sat in a larger chair on the other side. The desk was clear but there were large piles of paper around the room.

"What can I do for you?" he asked.

"We're pupils in Miss Loxley's class," began Marcus.

"Sarah told me that you knew her when she buzzed me from reception. I can give you both half an hour, if you've got something worthwhile to say."

Marcus was a little taken-aback by the man's manner. He had expected someone rather more like his form-teacher.

"We've started a campaign to save the railway line." Trudi spoke now.

"From Royds Well to Banham?"

"Yes."

"Then you must be the two youngsters who've gained notoriety in the local newspaper."

"Yes."

"Have you been expelled yet?"

"No," replied Trudi, "but we've learned not to trust journalists too much."

"I've had many good experiences of reporters and a few bad ones" said the businessman, "Their job is to tell us what's going on. Most do it well. My daughter is a foreign correspondent and my son works for a local paper. I'm proud of them both but I think the man at the Recorder betrayed your trust." He paused, leaving Trudi to regret her remark, before asking: "How can I help your campaign?"

"Do you have any influence on the railway company?"

"None at all. My company makes components for motor cars and all of them leave the factory by road."

"You wouldn't be able to persuade them to keep the line open, then?"

"I wouldn't even try," replied Mike Stephens. "Why do you want to save it, anyway?"

All of this seemed very unhelpful to Marcus and Trudi, who were wondering if they should now thank the businessman for his time and return home. Still, they remembered that Miss Loxley had asked them to see this man and decided that they ought to stay, for her sake.

"It's a lovely steam engine," said Marcus, "and those carriages…"

"I agree, but there are a lot of fine steam engines in museums. You will also realise that if the railway company changes its mind and keeps the line open, they will be running diesels on it in two years' time anyway. They are phasing out all stream trains."

"Trains carry a lot of people," argued Trudi. "That keeps those people off the roads."

"How full are the trains when they run from Banham to Royds Well?"

"Well - not very full," admitted Marcus, who felt as though their argument was being pulled apart piece by piece.

"Are the buses full?" asked the businessman.

"I've not been on them very often," replied Trudi, "but there weren't many people on the bus last time I did."

"So the people riding on the train could fill up the seats on the buses?

"I suppose they could," replied Trudi, "but the buses fill up the roads - trains don't. In a few years' time, the roads might become so full of traffic that the vehicles hardly move. People might want to use trains again then, but they won't be able to if the track has all been pulled up."

"How many years do you think that will be?" Mike Stephens continued to throw awkward questions at them.

"I can't say how many." Trudi was feeling irritated now. "I just know that my Father says there were very few cars on the road twenty years ago - and look at the number now."

"All right." The businessman nodded. "I'm running a business here. I've got to show my shareholders that I can make a profit this year, not at some unspecified time in the distant future."

"We realise that the railway has got to pay for itself too," Marcus contributed.

Mike Stephens suddenly laughed. "You two impress me very much," he said. "You don't give up, do you? You seem to see yourselves as some sort of guardians of the railway."

Trudi grinned, 'I like that. We're *Guardians of the Railway*, Marcus!"

"I didn't intend that to be a compliment," said Mike Stephens, quietly. "You're a couple of nuisances." He added with a twinkle in his eye.

There was silence. Neither of the schoolfriends knew how to react to this remark.

"It so happens," he said, "that I am very interested in trains myself. I've read all the articles in the local paper about the closure and I bet the railway company doesn't like your campaign and I've wondered whether it was necessary. You two might give me an excuse to find out."

"How do you mean?" asked Marcus.

"The railway company is presumably closing the line because they are not making enough money from it. That may be because it is badly managed. If I could buy that line and be sure that it wouldn't lose money, I should be very interested in it."

"Do you think that you could make money out of the line?" asked Trudi. This was the first glimmer of hope they had seen in their campaign.

"I don't know. I would need to see the figures about the costs of running the line and the income from it."

"Surely the railway company wouldn't show you that?" asked Marcus.

"They'll show me the figures," replied the businessman, "and I'm fairly confident that they'll show them to me on Monday morning.

I'm interested in buying the line and the railway company knows that I can afford it."

The schoolfriends looked at Mike Stephens, astonished. He wasn't joking.

"So where does that leave our campaign?" asked Marcus.

"I'm afraid," replied the businessman, "that you know very well where your campaign is. If you get more publicity in the local paper and on television, you will find it impossible not to link the name of the school with the campaign, causing further embarrassment to the school. You already know that if that happens, you will be expelled."

"Surely, as Chairman of Governors, you understand what we are trying to do?" pleaded Marcus.

"Yes. I also know that Mrs Hampshire has had to explain herself to the local council as a result of the publicity you have attracted to the school and she has had to promise that she would put a stop to it."

"Why?" asked Trudi.

"The school is there for everybody's children," replied Mike Stephens. "The director of the railways could send his child to Royds Well High if he wanted - the school does not have opinions about railway lines or anything else."

For the first time, Marcus and Trudi now understood why the Headmistress had been so appalled by the publicity they had given the school. The businessman changed the subject: "What time is your lunch break at school on Monday?"

Marcus told him.

"I see. You get an hour and a half. It would take you – what? Ten minutes to walk here?"

"Probably less than that," said Trudi.

"Meet me here at the start of your lunch break," said Mike Stephens. "I should be able to tell you then whether I can do anything to help you. In the meantime, not a word about this to anybody, understood?"

The two friends nodded.

"What about our school dinner?" asked Marcus.

Mike Stephens laughed: "You mean you would miss it? I was going to offer you a meal here. I thought you might prefer it."

So that was agreed. The schoolfriends left feeling confident that their new friend could save the railway line if anybody could.

"He's quite a character, isn't he?" said Marcus as they walked back to the station.

"He certainly is," agreed Trudi. "When he was asking all those awkward questions, I really thought he wasn't going to help us."

"Yes. I was wondering why Miss Loxley suggested that we speak to him."

"So you see - she was right," said Trudi.

Marcus laughed, "Do you want to see how to run a real railway? The one in my garden shed?"

Trudi did. When they were back at Marcus' house, he made cups of cocoa which they took with them into the shed.

Trudi had seen the model railway once before - on the Saturday afternoon two weeks previously when she had apologised to Marcus, but she found it just as impressive on the second occasion.

The lights on the stations, trains and on the signals, fascinated her. The houses, roads and cars in the village seemed so life-like that she could almost imagine herself living there.

Trudi noticed a steam train and a diesel standing next to one another at the station.

"I'm not sure that's realistic," she protested. "The Flying Scotsman and the Blue Pullman would hardly be on neighbouring platforms."

He stuck his tongue out at her. "If you want to run a railway, get your own." he grinned.

Just then, Mrs Redlands stuck her head round the door. "Really, Marcus," she exclaimed. "You are rude to your guests."

"She stuck her tongue out at me once," he argued, remembering the occasion on the railway station.

"I find that impossible to believe," replied Mrs Redlands firmly, smiling at Trudi. "Really – the things that girl has to put up with! Would you like to stay for lunch, Trudi? I'll phone your Dad and tell him if you do."

"Yes, please, if Marcus doesn't mind." she replied eagerly.

"Marcus doesn't mind," said his Mother.

When Mrs Redlands had left the shed and was out of earshot, Trudi turned to Marcus.

"Really, the things this girl has to put up with!" she said with a grin.

"You and my Mother make a formidable pair," he replied. "I'm going to have to make sure you don't see too much of each other, Do you want to run the Flying Scotsman?"

"What about the Blue Pullman?" she teased, so he gave her the controller for that.

"I'll take the Flying Scotsman later," she told him.

"Do you want the keys to my shed while you're at it?" he asked good-humouredly, holding it up in his hand.

Trudi made as if to take it. "Now you come to mention it, Marcus…"

The friends had a most amusing morning playing with the train set and hardly wanted to break off from it at lunchtime.

They did break off, of course and Trudi enjoyed Mrs Redlands' company. She talked about all sorts of things - everything it seemed, except the problems Marcus and Trudi had been having at school lately - and listened to the other two as well. Trudi didn't want the meal to finish.

In the afternoon the two friends spent a few more minutes in the shed with the model railway before returning to the house to play some hilarious board games with Marcus' Mother.

If, while enjoying themselves, Marcus and Trudi remembered the time when they had got into trouble and weren't allowed to see one another, they were determined that should never happen again...

Chapter 17

He Gives His Verdict

For the Guardians of the Railway – they hadn't thought of that description themselves, but both agreed they loved it – Monday morning was not their favourite time of the week.

This occasion, however, it seemed different. They would be seeing their new friend again at lunchtime and they would discover the fate of the railway.

Neither doubted that Mike Stephens would be able to save the railway. The millionaire would be using his money of course, but they could feel satisfaction that it had been their idea (with a little credit due to Miss Loxley!) Of course, there were four lessons to get through before the meeting - as Marcus kindly reminded Trudi as they stepped off the train.

"Don't get yourself so excited that you can't concentrate in lessons," he said. "Remember what happened last time."

"Why are you always telling me how to behave these days?" she asked, amused. She did though, intend to heed the warning. She didn't want all her teachers complaining to Miss Loxley again.

At lunchtime, the two friends were the first to return to their classrooms with their schoolbags.

"I understand that you two went to see Mike Stephens on Saturday. He told me that you were very polite and well-behaved - a real credit to the school," said Miss Loxley.

"Thank you, Miss." said Marcus and Trudi in chorus.

"Of course," added the form-mistress with a twinkle in her eye. "I didn't tell him what a pair of troublemakers you really are."

"We're going to see him again now," Trudi told her.

"I hope he's able to help you then," replied Miss Loxley. "You certainly deserve to succeed with all your hard work."

The two pupils had now put down their bags at their desks and had begun to race towards the door.

"Don't run," called the form-mistress, wondering whether she should have repeated the compliment.

Marcus and Trudi slowed down but only until they were out of her sight. Two more members of staff reminded them to walk in school before they were safely off the premises.

"We've escaped," grinned Trudi as they passed out of the school gates.

"With only a few tellings-off," smiled Marcus. "It's funny how I always seem to get into bother when I'm with you."

"Of all the cheek!" exclaimed Trudi. "You've got into less trouble since you've known me." This was probably true. Marcus seemed to be concentrating much more on his lessons these days.

The friends arrived at the reception of MS Engineering and were about to announce themselves when Mike Stephens appeared.

"I saw you from my office," he said. "Follow me." Turning to the receptionist, he added, "Sarah, could you ask the canteen to send some tomato soup to my office for the three of us? We can order our main course when we're there."

They hardly seemed to have sat down in the office before the soup arrived, along with a menu. They ordered their main courses.

"This soup is delicious," said Trudi. "Not like our school dinners."

The businessman laughed. "I didn't think you'd miss your school dinner. We have a very good canteen here, though I usually just have a sandwich at my desk. So it's a treat for me, too."

They continued to eat the soup in silence. Marcus and Trudi were desperate to know what their new friend would say about the railway, but they did not dare to ask. He would tell them in his own good time.

"There you are, my dears." The same kindly lady who had brought the soup took away the empty bowls and gave them their main courses.

As they began to tuck into their meals, the two friends looked expectantly at Mike Stephens. For the first time since they had met him, he looked slightly awkward.

"I've looked over the figures from the railway company," he said. "I can understand why they want to close the branch line."

"Why?" asked Trudi.

"They're losing a lot of money on it. They are just not getting enough passengers to pay the cost of running the line."

"How much does it cost to run the line?" asked Trudi.

Mike Stephens studied his visitors carefully before replying, "I've got all the figures here. I'm not supposed to show them to anyone, but if I do, you must promise me that you will keep everything you see a secret."

"We promise," replied the friends solemnly.

"Make sure you keep that promise." The businessman handed a sheet of figures to each of them.

Trudi and Marcus looked at the figures. They could see what Mike Stephens had meant. The railway line cost nearly three times as much to run as it was collecting in fares from passengers. A lot of the trains were almost empty. Only the trains which the friends caught to and from school, and some which ran at lunchtime, were carrying a reasonable number of people.

"The railway company would sell me the line for next-to-nothing," said Mike Stephens. "They'd throw in the station at Banham too. I was quite surprised. I think they must have had a lot of letters complaining about the closure. Your campaign has obviously been successful."

He paused, then continued, "I would have paid a lot more money than they are asking to buy the line, but as I said, I cannot afford to pay its debts if it is going to run at a loss. On these figures, it would."

"What are the costs?" asked Trudi.

"There's the cost of running and maintaining the engine and carriages, of course. There is an engine driver, a station master at Banham and we would have to pay part of the wages of the ticket inspector at Royds Well."

"Why do we have to pay part of the wages for someone at Royds Well station?"

Mike Stephens grinned. "Somebody needs to check and collect the tickets for people getting off the train there Trudi, or they might have been riding on it without paying. Most of the trains at Royds Well station are going in the other direction, to Dunston, but they say that one in ten of the trains is on your line. So they think we should pay a tenth of the ticket inspector's wages."

The others said nothing. It was difficult to see where they could save money.

"Any chance that we could increase the number of passengers?" asked Marcus.

The businessman looked serious: "I wish we could," he replied, "but this line has been losing passengers for more than twenty years. We can't suddenly treble the numbers."

"It's ridiculous," Trudi burst out. "In a few years' time, the roads are going to be overcrowded and then people will want to use the railways again. Here we are trying to save this railway line and it seems that we can do nothing about it."

"That seems to be the size of it."

"You're sure we can do nothing," pressed Marcus.

"I can only afford to buy that line if it can pay its own running costs. At the moment, it doesn't."

"So what happens now?" asked Trudi.

"I've expressed an interest in buying the line. I've seen the figures, and as they are at the moment, I couldn't possibly buy it. Unless we can think of a way of keeping the line open - and we need to do it quickly or somebody's going to buy the station, knock it down and build a supermarket there. If the station goes, we have no chance of saving the railway."

This was a very gloomy thought and the others didn't know what to say.

"Pudding anyone?" Mike Stephens broke the silence.

"Yes, please."

As they ate their pudding, the three did not talk about the railway line anymore. Mike Stephens had not said it would be impossible to save the railway line, but it now looked very unlikely.

When they had finished their meal, Trudi glanced at her watch and noticed with alarm that school was due to start again in five minutes.

"Don't worry," said the businessman. "I'll give you a lift back."

So they rode back to school in a smart black Jaguar - and Marcus was very jealous that Trudi sat in the front seat.

"I won't drop you in front of the school gates in case your friends see you," said Mike Stephens, not that Marcus and Trudi would have minded!

They got out of the car in the next street and soon they were through the school gates.

"How did you get on?" asked Miss Loxley.

"Not very well," said Marcus gloomily. "I don't think he can do anything."

"I'm sorry," she replied, and the two friends knew that she meant it.

Rather like the day they had first learned of the railway closure, Trudi found it hard to concentrate that afternoon. She was thinking about the meeting that lunchtime. It all seemed so unfair. On Saturday, she had been convinced, like Marcus, that Mike Stephens would rescue the railway. Now, it seemed that wouldn't happen and all their efforts over the past fortnight had been wasted...

"Have you come here to learn French or sit there with your own private thoughts?"

Mrs Boyd's sharp question reminded her of the lesson she was in. "Sorry, Miss."

"Then perhaps you could answer the question I asked you?"

"What was that, Miss?"

"Really, Trudi..." The whole afternoon was like that.

Trudi would think momentarily about French, English and Maths, but then the railway took over.

Somehow, it seemed more important, to the pupil, if not to her teachers...

Chapter 18

New Ideas

Two gloomy pupils stepped off the train at Banham that evening. Marcus and Trudi found it difficult to smile now they felt they had lost their battle.

"You two don't look very happy." The sight of Sid Parkes could cheer them up at any time - and especially now.

"We're not," replied Trudi. "We thought we had a plan to save the railway, but we don't think it's going to work."

"Tell you what," said the old railwayman. "Why don't I make you a cup of cocoa in my office and you can tell me all about it?"

The two friends happily agreed to this suggestion.

"I'll be with you when I've checked the other tickets," said Sid. "Give me five minutes."

"At least we've got one loyal friend," said Marcus when they were in the office.

Trudi nodded her head in agreement.

A moment or so later Sid came through the door and closed it. "I gather you haven't saved the railway yet, then?"

"No," replied Trudi glumly. "We held a demonstration, got ourselves in the local newspaper and on television, nearly got ourselves expelled from school - that didn't work..."

"You're being hard on yourselves," said the old railwayman.

"How do you mean, Sid?" cut in Marcus.

"I mean," replied the station master, "that you have ruffled a lot of feathers at our regional office. They've closed lots of branch lines over the last few years, you know, and they've never once had a campaign against it."

"Would that make a difference to them?" asked Trudi.

"They won't keep the line open if it continues to lose money - that hasn't changed - but they are now willing to sell it if they can find a buyer."

"We thought we'd found somebody who would buy it," said Marcus. "Mike Stephens of MS Engineering in Royds Well. He told us he would get the figures from the railway company and study them over the weekend. He was willing to buy the line, but it would have to pay its own running costs."

"... and he doesn't like the figures?"

"That's about the size of it."

"I'm not surprised."

"Why do you say that?" Trudi was astonished by the railwayman's comment.

"Because this line can't be taking half the amount in fares that it costs to run."

Trudi nearly blurted out "just over a third, actually," but stopped herself in time. Mike Stephens had warned them not to repeat that information. Instead, she asked: "Is there any way of cutting costs or increasing the passengers?"

"You're not going to increase passengers much in the near future, bearing in mind how much they have dropped in recent years. As to the costs, you've got my wages and the wages of the driver. Of course, the engines, carriages and track also have to be maintained."

He paused, then added in a low voice, "I probably shouldn't be saying this - I wouldn't say it if I wasn't about to retire - but I haven't much to do these days. There are only four trains going out of here between the start of the morning and lunchtime and I sell the tickets to the passengers for those. I also check tickets and collect them for people getting off here. The train takes half an hour to get to Royds Well, spends ten minutes there and takes half an hour to get back. I'm not really doing much during the hour or so there is no train in the station here, except keeping the station tidy. Of course, it wasn't always like that," he concluded sadly. "This was a busy station once."

"You're saying it's hopeless, then, aren't you?" asked Marcus.

"Not hopeless, no. To save this railway, you would probably need to reduce it to four services a day; the train you catch to Royds Well in the morning, and one back from there at lunchtime. Send that train back to Royds Well in the early afternoon, and it can bring you back home from school in the evening."

"That would make money?"

"Not on its own, Miss. You'd have to get rid of my job and see whether the driver could drive some trains out of Royds Well, when he wasn't needed on this line."

"Who would do your job?" Trudi enquired.

"I'm retiring next March, don't forget."

"Somebody needs to sell the tickets and check them for the trains which come in?"

"Are there any teachers at your school who are interested in railways?"

"It's got to be a volunteer, then?"

"The railway company won't keep the line open as it is. They would very happily have sold this station so that somebody could build a supermarket on it, you know - they would have got a lot of money for it.

Your campaign has stopped them, for the moment at least, that's the only reason they're willing to sell the line."

"So we've done something but not enough," said Trudi slowly. "It's not just a matter of finding a buyer for the railway, it's got to be re-organised as well."

"That's it," said the old railwayman.

"Is it worth it?" asked Marcus.

"You've got to answer that for yourself, young man," replied Sid, "but when you first came to see me the young lady was pointing out how much traffic there is on the roads now, and how that is likely to grow. If this line closes, they'll probably take up the track and demolish the station. Then you'll never get it back."

Marcus and Trudi knew all that; they had used the same arguments in their letter to the paper. Marcus sighed: "You're right, you know," he said. "I just wonder if we can sell the idea to Mike Stephens."

The railwayman grinned: "Give yourself credit for what you have achieved so far," he said. "If it wasn't for you, the station might already have been sold. There was a supermarket company which was very interested in buying it, but they've pulled out. You might succeed yet."

The two friends smiled and Trudi gave Sid a hug. He might well be right. Even if he wasn't, he had certainly cheered them up…

"Call round at eight o'clock," shouted Marcus as they left the station a few minutes later than usual. "We must discuss this. I'll be in the shed."

Trudi was feeling very excited as she walked home that evening. Sid might have told them how to save the railway, but it all seemed very complicated. Could they find volunteers to sell tickets at Banham in the morning and at lunchtime? They would also need somebody to check and sell tickets at Royds Well if the Banham line would now be separate from the other trains running out of that station. Even if they did that, Sid had said that the engine driver would have to spend part of his time working for the railway company. Could that be arranged?

So excited was Trudi that she completely forgot about her Geography homework, though she remembered to do her French and Maths. She was at Marcus' house at five to eight, just as he was finishing his homework.

"We'll go to the shed," he called to his Mother as he put his pen down. "We won't disturb you there."

"… and I suppose I won't disturb you either," laughed Mrs Redlands. "Alright you two, I'll give you some peace…"

"Thanks, Mum." Marcus gave her a hug. "You're the best."

"Now I'm really suspicious about what you're going to talk about," said his Mother with a twinkle in her eye.

Once they were in the shed, Marcus switched on the railway and gave Trudi control of the "Flying Scotsman."

"So what do we do now?" he asked.

"About the real railway?"

He nodded.

"I think Sid is probably right. The railway can't go on as it is - the four trains he mentioned are probably the only ones which carry a reasonable number of passengers. The others will have to be cut out - and we're going to have to find volunteers to do Sid's job."

Marcus nodded again. He had come to the same conclusion. "When do we tell Mike Stephens?"

"Could we write a note asking to see him on Saturday?" asked Trudi. "I don't want another lunchtime meeting - I couldn't concentrate on my work this afternoon."

"I noticed," said Marcus. "So did the teachers, I'm afraid." Trudi blushed. Until just over a couple of weeks ago, she hadn't been used to getting into trouble at school.

"You've got to watch it, you know, Trudi," he said gently. "You won't help to save the railway by getting into bother all the time."

"Who do you think you are - one of the teachers?" Trudi suddenly burst out. "I'm going home - I've had enough of this." She had stood up and was out of the shed door before Marcus had grasped what was happening.

He tried to run after her. "Trudi, TRUDI!" he called, as she walked along the drive towards the road. She only quickened her pace. Marcus had never seen Trudi so angry. He had assumed that they were firm friends after all they had been through, and now she had walked out on him.

He stopped, wondering what to do. If he chased her, she would run all the faster, and he knew from the time they had been in the park that she was quicker than he was. There was no point in that, but he had to put the matter right that evening.

"Whatever has happened?" asked Mrs Redlands, suddenly appearing out of the back door. She must have heard Marcus calling to Trudi.

"She just suddenly blew a fuse," he answered. "One minute she was there, next minute she had gone."

"What were you doing, Marcus?"

"Trying to give her some advice," he replied, a little shame-facedly.

"I expect she'll be over it in the morning," said Mrs Redlands kindly.

"I can't wait until the morning. I've got to go there now and apologise," Marcus replied urgently.

"Alright but give her the time to get home and cool off," urged his Mother.

Marcus could see the wisdom of this, but he didn't want to wait too long.

"I'll give her ten minutes."

He returned to the shed and switched off the model railway. Then he stared into space.

Marcus had never been certain that they could save the railway, though it was beginning to look as if they might. He had been sure that he and Trudi would be firm friends from now on, whatever happened. He was completely bewildered by Trudi's outburst a few minutes before.

Trudi was lying on her bed. Tears had welled up in her eyes as she left the shed, but she had only spoken to her Father briefly when she got back to the house and he hadn't noticed. At least, she hoped he hadn't.

She had picked up *'Emma's Adventures'*, which usually took her mind off any problems. This evening, though, she simply saw words swimming about on the page. Things had started to go wrong at school again when Trudi thought she had put all of that behind her.

Then Marcus - with his record - had chosen to remind her about it, to tease her about it even. Of one thing Trudi was certain. She didn't want to see Marcus again, not ever...

Chapter 19

More Trouble

It was just before half-past eight when Marcus knocked on the door of Trudi's home.

Mr Barnes greeted him warmly. "Come in," he said. "I expect you'll want to see Trudi, she got back a few minutes ago. I thought she'd gone to see you actually."

Marcus smiled and entered the house. He was relieved that Trudi had apparently said nothing to her Father about storming out, but he wondered how she would react when she saw him. He would know soon enough.

Mr Barnes knocked on Trudi's bedroom door. "Marcus is here to see you. Shall I send him up?"

"Tell him that I'm in bed, Dad." Trudi had asked her Father to tell a lie before she realised what she had said. Mr Barnes was surprised but chose not to comment. It was early but perhaps his daughter was very tired this evening. He told Marcus.

The boy walked down the drive to the road and stopped. He didn't believe what Trudi had just told her Father - and he had to see her that night if possible.

He remembered the night Trudi had sneaked out of the house and walked to the park. When they got back, she had shinned up the tree and moved along the branch with her arms, until she got to the window. Could he do that now? Would the branch bear his weight? He wasn't going to stand around thinking about it.

A moment later he had climbed the tree and put first one hand then the other on the branch and was edging towards Trudi's window. The curtains were drawn at the front of the house and he hoped that Mr Barnes would not have heard him as he walked towards the back of the house. Very carefully, with one hand still on the branch, he tapped on the window with the other. Trudi opened the drawn curtains and motioned to him to go away. He tapped again, hoping that she would open the window quickly.

He did not want to stay in this precarious position for long. Trudi drew the curtains again. Marcus tapped the window a little harder, one last time. Trudi flung back the curtains and opened the window. "What on earth do you want?" she asked, her eyes flashing.

"To come in first of all," he replied. "Then perhaps I can explain myself."

Looking not at all pleased, Trudi moved away from the window and allowed him entry.

"Whatever is the matter?" he asked, sitting himself down on the floor. "One minute we were in my shed enjoying ourselves and the next you had stormed out on me."

"It's you," she almost screamed. "You're enjoying this, aren't you? It's ever so funny to see the girl who had never put a foot wrong get into so much trouble. You admitted that yourself once."

"I said no such thing." replied Marcus firmly.

"I never used to be in bother at school before I met you, now I can't seem to stay out of it. I thought these problems were behind me, but they started again today. I expect Mrs Hampshire will be writing to my Father soon - and it's ALL YOUR FAULT!" wailed Trudi.

"Excuse me," cut in Marcus, now extremely irritated. "I seem to remember that we both agreed to try to save the railway. Yes, we've made mistakes and we've had problems with the school but I'm not taking all the blame for that."

"Go away," she shouted. "I'm fed up with you laughing at me. I don't want to speak to you again."

"I'm not laughing at anyone..."

"GO. AWAY."

"Alright, I'm not staying when I'm not wanted." Marcus climbed out of the window and carefully took hold of the branch, first with one hand and then the other. "You might be interested to know, Trudi Barnes, that when I first sat opposite you on the train, I thought you were a stuck-up little goody two-shoes. I still do."

Trudi slammed the window shut and Marcus edged carefully along the branch. The girl had already drawn the curtains. Mr Barnes, who had heard the sound of voices, rushed up to her room. "What was that?"

"It was Marcus. He was talking to me from the garden," Trudi lied and immediately despised herself for it. She told herself that she would never have done such a thing before she met Marcus.

"Your conversation didn't sound too friendly."

"We'll work through it, Dad." That was an even bigger lie but Trudi did not wish to discuss her relations with Marcus just now.

"I hope you do. He's a nice lad."

When her Father had left the room, Trudi decided to go to bed. She turned her light out, lay down on her pillow - and wept.

Marcus, half-way home, was cursing to himself. Whatever had made him say those stupid things to Trudi as he left? Now, they might never be friends again.

"Did you make up with Trudi?" asked his Mother kindly when he got home.

"Not quite - I think I made things worse."

"Well, I should patch it up if I were you. She's a nice girl."

Away from the heat of the argument he had had with her, Marcus did not need any persuading of this, but he believed that he had blown it.

The following morning - Tuesday - Marcus and Trudi sat at opposite ends of the railway carriage. He had said "Good Morning" to her, but she had simply replied: "Do you say that to many stuck-up little goody two-shoes, then?"

Geography was the fourth lesson of the morning, and the elderly, grey-haired and somewhat fearsome Mr Moss began his lesson promptly.

"Right, you will pass your exercise books to the front of the class, so that I can mark your homework, and I will give you a little test on the pages I asked you to read last night." He started to hand out pieces of paper for the test.

Trudi realised with horror that she had not done her Geography homework, the one subject she wasn't good at. She put her hand up and realised that it was shaking.

"Yes, Barnes?"

"Please, sir, I forgot to do my homework."

"I beg your pardon!" The teacher was standing almost on top of her now. "Perhaps you would like to explain to your classmates why you forgot to do your homework - when they obviously didn't?"

Marcus watched this scene, horrified. He bore Trudi no ill will, he had said worse things to Trudi last night than she had said to him and he knew what agony it must be to her to be humiliated like this. He would rather that this bully had picked on him than Trudi.

"It just... slipped my mind." The schoolgirl was close to tears.

"*It – just - slipped - your - mind.*" The teacher repeated the words slowly. "It's strange how this railway business never just slips your mind, you manage to get yourself in the newspaper every week about it. Perhaps you and I ought to have a little chat at the end of the lesson before you go to lunch, so that it doesn't - just - slip - your - mind again." Mr Moss turned to the rest of the class. "Right, the pantomime is over. Those of you who have actually done some work can do the test, now that I've collected your books."

So Trudi sat reading her textbook, her face red with embarrassment as the others did the test. It was an agonising forty-five minutes and she would happily have fallen through a hole in the floor. However, she did not wish the time away - she was looking forward even less to the 'little chat' afterwards.

The buzzer rang at the end of the lesson, passing through Trudi like a bolt of electricity. She was on her own, now, with Mr Moss. "Barnes will stay behind." he announced, as if she needed reminding.

Marcus wished he could have stayed in the room to protect Trudi. Instead, he decided to wait outside.

"Now then, young lady," said Mr Moss in a cold, quiet voice when he had shut the door and the others had gone. "Perhaps you can tell me why you forgot your Geography homework?"

"I had my mind on the railway." Trudi decided she might as well tell the truth.

"I see. The railway is more important than your Geography homework?"

There was a sneer in the man's voice.

Trudi suddenly snapped. "As it happens, it is to me," she replied. "I haven't any more time to waste talking to you - I'm going." With that, she marched to the door and walked out of the room, slamming the door behind her.

When he had quite recovered, Mr Moss followed her out of the door.

"BARNES! Come back here this minute!" he shouted.

Trudi did not turn her head. Mr Moss started to chase her but she put on a sprint, and he knew he was beaten.

She did not feel like any lunch now and besides, she was late anyway; she went into the playground instead.

Marcus had watched Trudi leave the room, followed by Mr Moss. He was amused to think how startled the old teacher would be by Trudi's behaviour, when he probably thought of her as a girl 'who wouldn't say boo to a goose'. Yet Marcus felt guilty, too - Trudi's attitude today was probably because of what he had said the previous evening.

There might yet be very serious consequences for Trudi of her defiance of Mr Moss - she could even be expelled. He wondered whether to try to find her. No, she was still upset with him. Late as it was, he would go to lunch.

"Trudi Barnes." Miss Loxley looked more anxious than Marcus had ever seen her at afternoon registration. "The Headmistress wishes to see you. Now."

Trudi went to see Mrs Hampshire, as Marcus followed the rest of the class to the next lesson. Then he turned around.

"Tell Duffy I've got to see somebody," he told a trusted friend, before racing along the corridor towards the Headmistress' study. The door was just closing as he got there. He knelt down to listen at the keyhole, hoping that no members of staff would happen to walk along in the next few minutes.

"I gather from Mr Moss that you were extremely rude to him this morning. He says that you forgot your homework and he asked you to stay behind for five minutes so that he could speak to you about it. You then told him that, as far as you were concerned, saving the railway was far more important than Geography homework and you weren't going to waste your time listening to him. You ran out of his classroom, ignoring his calls to you to come back, and he was unable to catch you. Is this true?" Mrs Hampshire spoke sharply.

"Yes, Miss."

"Are you willing to apologise to Mr Moss?"

"No, Miss."

"Trudi, you and Marcus have caused both me and this school a lot of trouble since you started your campaign to save the railway. I have had several nasty letters and telephone calls since the article was published in the local paper last Friday. Despite that, I have tried to protect you from the anger of a lot of my staff and Governors. I can't protect you from this stupidity, if you won't help yourself. Let me ask you again. Will you apologise?"

"No." shouted Trudi defiantly. "Mr Moss is a bully. He made me look a fool in front of the class. It was awful. I'm not saying sorry."

"Let's not play games any longer, Trudi. You're going to apologise to Mr Moss for being rude to him or I shall suspend you from school immediately for a week. Unless you are willing to say sorry at the end of that time, I will have no choice." She paused. "I will recommend to the Governors that you are expelled. I don't want to do it, Trudi, but defying my staff is a very serious matter. I'll ask you one more time. Will you say sorry?"

"No," replied Trudi quietly.

"Then we have nothing more to say to one another," said Mrs Hampshire. "Trudi, I am very sorry it has come to this. I wish you well in your next school."

Trudi stood up, feeling as if the whole situation was unreal. She looked at the Headmistress' study, aware that this was probably the last time she would see it. Indeed, this might well be the last day she was at Royds Well High - she could hardly believe it.

Yet she could not bring herself to apologise to Mr Moss...

Chapter 20

Calmer Waters

There was a knock on the door.

"Come in," called the Headmistress. As Trudi was about to leave, Marcus entered.

"I think Trudi had better stay," he said. "I've got something to say and I want her to hear it."

"Then you'd both better sit down. Trudi is in serious trouble - as you will no doubt know if you have been listening at the door." Mrs Hampshire spoke coldly.

"I guessed as much," replied Marcus, not wishing to admit that he had been eavesdropping. "You see, she and I had an argument last night and I called her a nasty name."

"What was the name?"

"I'm ashamed of it now and I don't want to repeat it." he said.

"Is this true?" The Headmistress turned to Trudi, who nodded.

She was furious that Marcus was interfering - didn't he think she could handle her own problems?

"Alright, Marcus. What has this got to do with me?"

"Well, I believe that Trudi was a little rude to Mr Moss."

"How would you know that?"

"I - overheard it, Miss."

"Is it your habit Marcus, of listening at everybody's door?"

"No, Miss." He blushed. "It's just that I feel responsible for Trudi's behaviour - I think she was very upset. That's probably why she forgot her Geography homework - it's certainly why she spoke to Mr Moss like that."

There was silence for what seemed like an age. At last, the Headmistress broke it with a sigh. "Defying a member of my staff, and speaking rudely to a member of my staff, are two matters which I take very seriously. I suppose, Marcus, I had better believe you. Certainly I have had no complaint of this sort about Trudi before and nor would I have expected it."

She turned to Trudi, "By rights, I should still insist on that apology."

"Mr Moss was nasty to her Miss. He showed her up in front of the whole class, and then she had to sit there for the next forty-five minutes. It was awful."

"Thank you, Marcus. Mr Moss can be a little difficult at times - perhaps he feels that things aren't the same in schools as they once were - but pupils must accept his authority."

She paused: "On this occasion Trudi, I am going to say that you didn't do your homework and you were rude because you were feeling unwell. It must never happen again."

Trudi nodded.

"Have you had any lunch?"

The girl shook her head.

"Nor have I," said the Headmistress. "I'll order some from the kitchens. We'll have something to eat and then I'm driving you home."

She glanced at Marcus. "As for you, young man, you're supposed to be in Mrs Duffy's class, aren't you? I'll give you a note apologising for your lateness and saying I wanted to see you. As you have said that you should be blamed for Trudi's rudeness..." She hesitated.

"Yes, Miss?"

"You'll spend half an hour after school picking up litter in the playground."

"But... I'll miss my train home."

"You needn't worry about that. I'll give you a lift home and explain to your Mother that you've had to do important duties after school."

"Thank you, Miss."

"That's quite alright. I don't think you'll be very late, and you can spend your half hour remembering that it's a bad idea to call a girl names." The Headmistress seemed quite chirpy now.

Trudi grinned at Marcus. Perhaps their friendship was restored after all…

At that moment there was another knock on the door. It was Mr Moss.

"Ah, Mr Moss, do come in and join the party." said Mrs Hampshire cheerfully.

"I trust that you have punished that girl very severely?" said the teacher.

"As it happens Mr Moss, I haven't. Trudi has been feeling unwell yesterday evening and today. That is why she didn't do her homework and it also explains her… outburst… this lunchtime."

"That's what she told you, is it?"

"It is, Mr Moss, and I happen to believe her. I shall be taking her home myself in a few minutes, but she has something to say to you first."

Trudi stood up. "I'm sorry, sir." she said meekly.

"Very well," he replied.

"Well," said the Headmistress. "Trudi has apologised to you Mr Moss. I'm sure there will be no need to refer to this unfortunate incident again."

"Indeed not." he replied, not sounding convinced.

"Thank you, Mr Moss. If there's nothing else?"

The teacher left the Headmistress's office.

"Right, then," said Mrs Hampshire. "I must slip away for a couple of minutes. I will leave you together in case you have anything to say to each other. Then we'll have dinner, Trudi."

"Thank you, Miss."

When Mrs Hampshire had left the room, closing the door behind her, Trudi stood up. "Thanks, Marcus. You've really saved my bacon." Then she looked serious again. "You didn't mean what you said last night?"

He stood up too and laughed. "Of course I didn't. You're the nicest person I know - how could I think that of you?"

She gave him a hug.

"Anyway, I'd better go," he said. "I don't want to miss too much of old Duffy's lesson - even for your sake."

Trudi giggled: "You won't forget your important duties this evening, will you?"

"No I won't, Trudi. I deserved that."

"Perhaps." Trudi smiled, then looked serious: "I'm to blame too though, Marcus. I said that you enjoyed seeing me get into trouble and that was unfair." She gave him another hug before he left for his lesson.

Lunch with Mrs Hampshire proved to be a very pleasant experience. She even asked what was happening with the railway but Trudi was glad to be home. Perhaps at last her problems at school were over and things might get back to normal.

That evening Marcus called and went up to Trudi's room - with her permission on this occasion, to speak to her. He checked that she had done all her homework, which she did not take amiss, and then they spent almost an hour discussing what to do about the railway.

They came back to Sid's ideas as probably the only way in which the line could be saved. They decided to visit Mike Stephens the following Saturday and put the new ideas to him. If he turned them down, that would be the end of their campaign. Trudi wrote a letter to the businessman asking if he would see them then. She and Marcus both signed it. On sudden impulse she wrote the words, 'Guardians of the Railway', after their names.

The following day – Wednesday - Trudi was nervous about returning to school after her recent problems, but she need not have been. The next three days passed very smoothly and all her teachers commented that she seemed to be fully recovered.

Even Mr Moss told both Miss Loxley and the Headmistress that he considered Trudi to be a very hardworking and serious student.

Saturday morning arrived at last. As the two friends travelled to Royds Well on the train, they were aware that it was now just over three weeks since the railway company announced the closure. If they were going to save the line, they needed to persuade Mike Stephens of their idea that day.

The businessman showed them into his office as before and, having shut the door behind him, said, "Alright, we agreed last time that I couldn't buy the railway as it is run at the moment because it wouldn't pay for itself. What suggestions have you got for me?"

The two pupils looked at one another. At last, Trudi broke the silence: "We agree that the railway is losing money at the moment. We've done a little research and we understand that the only trains which are reasonably full are the one we catch in the morning from Banham, the trains running to and from Banham at lunchtime, and the train we catch home from Royds Well in the evening. We think the small number of passengers for the other trains could use the bus."

The businessman nodded approvingly: "I'm impressed. Are all of these your ideas?"

Trudi grinned: "I wish they were. We've had a little help from a friend, but we're not sure he wants to take the credit."

"That's a shame," replied Mike Stephens, "but do carry on."

"Banham would not need a full-time Station Master with our new timetable," continued Trudi. "Volunteers could collect and sell tickets at the two stations when the trains were running, so we won't need to replace Sid Parkes when he retires."

"Good idea. That still leaves the problem of the train driver, though. The wages of the driver are more than the amount of money which the line is getting from passengers. How do you pay for him?"

Marcus spoke now. "We wondered whether the driver might be able to drive trains from say Royds Well to Dunston during the morning and afternoon, when he wasn't needed to drive the train to Banham."

"Those trains would still be run by the railway company," argued the businessman.

"Couldn't the cost of the driver be shared between the two?"

"It's an interesting thought." Mike Stephens looked earnest. "Yes, that would certainly cut the cost of running the railway. In fact, it might just tip the balance. If I can get the railway company to agree to share a driver with us, I might be able to buy the line." There was silence for a moment or so. To Marcus and Trudi, this was beyond their wildest dreams…

"Trudi, where do we find the volunteers?" The businessman broke the silence.

"School, I suppose. Some of the teachers might be willing to help."

"Alright, how does this sound? I'm prepared to buy the railway line and give it to the school if some of the teachers will help with the running of it."

Marcus and Trudi could have jumped for joy, this was brilliant news.

Mike Stephens looked serious. "The school would have to be willing to agree to take on the railway, of course…"

"Why wouldn't they?" asked Trudi.

"We seem to have a plan - at least, you and your friend thought of it - to make a profit on the railway. On the other hand, if the school owned it, and it lost money, they would be responsible for the debts."

"Is that likely?" asked Marcus.

"Very unlikely. I would expect the school to keep an eye on the cost of running the railway all the time, if they accept the gift of it from me, but they might be worried about it."

"When are you going to put it to them?" asked Trudi, her eyes shining.

"I'm not. You two are - at the Governor's meeting next Wednesday evening."

"*What?*" asked Marcus and Trudi together.

"You two are going to address the Governor's meeting. Don't worry - we'll agree beforehand what you are going to say, and I'm the one who will be buying the line. I think you'll make a good case to them - you've certainly persuaded me."

"If you think so," said Trudi doubtfully.

"I do," replied Mike Stephens. "One last thing which I want you to do…"

Being asked to ride to school on the bus on Monday morning was the last thing the friends expected. The request left them feeling baffled and hoping that the businessman was serious about all of this…

Chapter 21

The Governors' Meeting

The bus left Banham at the same time as the train on Monday morning and Marcus and Trudi obediently caught it, though they were still puzzled by the request.

The businessman telephoned each of them that evening.: "I trust you caught the bus to and from school today like I asked you."

"We did."

He asked the friends how full the bus had been. They told him that it had been less than half full in each direction. The bus took as long as the train to get from Banham to Royds Well, and it had left at the same times, so it made no difference to the young passengers. Of course, they would much rather ride on the lovely steam train...

Mike Stephens, in turn, told them what to say at the Governors' meeting. "I'll give you a lift there and back in the car," he said. "The meeting's at half-past seven."

Marcus' Mother and Trudi's Father were surprised that the youngsters were being asked to speak to the Governors and rang the businessman to check. He reassured them that he was serious.

Marcus and Trudi were told that they would have to wait outside the room where the meeting was being held until the railway was to be discussed.

Mike Stephens collected them on Wednesday evening, as promised, but did not talk about the railway as they drove to Royds Well. As he was going into the meeting, he said: "Just stick to the script we agreed. I've got a rabbit to pull out of the hat later."

Trudi and Marcus had no idea what he was talking about and could only trust him. They would discover soon enough whether they were right to do so...

At last, two very nervous pupils were called to speak to the Governors. Mrs Hampshire, who invited them in, smiled warmly. "I shall be very interested in what you have to say," she said.

The Headmistress introduced the Governors. Some were parents and there was a teacher, too.

Mike Stephens spoke. "The other Governors know that I am willing to buy the railway line and give it to the school, so the railway company doesn't close it down. I wanted Trudi and Marcus to speak to you, because I know how much that line means to them, and I want them to explain why."

He turned to the pupils, "I want you to imagine that you are speaking to your friends. Don't be nervous, please tell us why you wanted to save the railway."

Trudi began hesitantly: "We wanted to save the railway because it's so much fun riding on it. Most of our friends go to school in cars or on buses, or they walk if they live near enough. We're the only ones we know who ride on a train - and especially on a steam train."

"Marcus?" Mike Stephens prompted.

"I agree with everything Trudi has said, but we had other reasons too. A lot more people are using the roads these days - there isn't a problem yet, but there could be one day. People might decide that they want to use the railway again, but they won't be able to if the tracks have been taken up."

"The railway isn't paying its way at the moment. How would you get around that?" The businessman was fielding an easy question, the friends knew the answer.

"We propose a new timetable for it," said Trudi, passing a sheet of paper to each Governor. "You will see that we have kept the trains we catch in the morning and evening as they are.

"At lunchtime, a train will travel from Royds Well to Banham, ten minutes from the start of our lunch break, so that one of the teachers could collect the fares, and the train will be back at Royds Well ten minutes before the start of afternoon school."

"Who would collect the fares at Banham for the morning and afternoon services from there? The Station Master?" asked the Headmistress.

"No," replied Trudi. "He retires next March, and we can't afford to replace him - perhaps a teacher."

"I think we might be able to find one of those. Mr McCann lives in Banham and he's very interested in railways." Miss Loxley, who had been invited to the meeting to help put the pupils at their ease, spoke up.

"That would be alright in the morning. What about lunchtimes?" asked Mrs Hampshire.

"He might be willing to ride to Banham and back on the train then. If he isn't, I would be, and we might be able to form a rota with some of the other staff. I think this is a super idea." Jill Loxley was getting very enthusiastic now.

"So what would be the costs of running the line?" The Headmistress spoke to Marcus and Trudi as if they were accountants.

"We would have to pay the cost of maintaining the steam engine and carriages, and the cost of the driver. We hope that the driver might be able to work for the railway company too, so we could share the cost of the driver with them." Trudi felt confident now - she believed that they were going to persuade the Governors of their point of view.

"The railway would make money if those were the only costs?" Mrs Hampshire seemed determined to pursue this point.

"Yes." Mike Stephens answered this question.

"How much?"

The businessman passed round the accounts which he had shown to Marcus and Trudi at their second meeting. He also handed around some new figures, showing how much it would cost to run the line with the suggested changes.

"If we adopt your ideas, Trudi and Marcus, we might make some money for the school. What happens if the line loses money?"

Trudi looked uncomfortable: "The school would bear the loss. We would soon know if the line was losing money and I suppose, it would have to be closed."

"You're quite sure that wouldn't happen?"

"The figures show clearly that we can make this work."

Mike Stephens nodded enthusiastically: "I agree."

"This is a very interesting idea. I think we should congratulate Marcus and Trudi on their hard work," began the Headmistress.

The pupils looked anxiously at her. They had a nasty feeling she was about to turn down their ideas.

"I'm afraid, however, that I cannot recommend to the Governors that they accept the gift of the railway from Mr Stephens. There is a risk, however small, that it could lose money. If it does, this school can't afford it."

Mike Stephens looked round the room. "Perhaps some of the other Governors have a view on this?"

"I agree with Jennifer Hampshire," called out a parent. "There's just too much risk."

"We can't use money from this school to pay for losses on the railway," called out a well-dressed man. "It should be spent on our children's education."

All the other Governors nodded their heads in agreement. Trudi glanced at Mike Stephens, who winked. Surely the man could not talk his way out of this?

The Chairman of Governors grinned. "I had a feeling you would be worried about that," he said. "It so happens I was worried about that myself, too."

All eyes were now on Mike Stephens.

"I've spoken to the bus company. They don't get many passengers on any of the services which run at the times we want to run our trains, so they have agreed to stop running buses then. We should get the extra passengers on the train. In return, they want to take a fifth share of the railway line."

"So they take some of the profits?" asked the Headmistress.

"They'll take some of the profits yes, but if the line starts to lose money, they will pay any losses and take it off our hands."

"... and close it down?"

"If they have to, yes, but nobody is expecting that. We all think it's going to be a great success."

"So we've nothing to lose?" called out the woman parent Governor.

"Nothing at all," replied Mike Stephens triumphantly.

"Let's do it then," shouted the well-dressed man.

Trudi and Marcus could hardly believe it. The railway was not only going to be saved, it was going to be bought for the school.

The meeting had now finished and, as they filed out, many Governors congratulated Marcus and Trudi on their ideas. The pupils could hardly believe that these were the same people who according to Mrs Hampshire, had been baying for their blood a few days before. Last to leave were the Headmistress and Mike Stephens. Mrs Hampshire spoke to the pupils.

"You know," she said. "I'm very pleased with what you two have done here tonight. It will be marvellous for the school to own that railway line and I intend to make sure that as many people as possible get involved with it."

She paused, remembering that at times the friends had got into trouble for their campaign: "I *had* to ask the questions I did, you know. We couldn't have taken on a risk. Thanks to Mr Stephens, we won't be doing."

She paused again, then said: "Mr Stephens is of course, very generously paying for the line, but I know that this has happened because of your ideas about how it could be run."

Trudi knew it would be unfair for her and Marcus to take all the credit: "Actually, Miss, a very good friend of ours gave us a lot of the ideas, but he is very shy."

"Then I won't ask who he is," replied the Headmistress. "I also wanted to say that I hope there are no hard feelings between us, I know that we were in conflict about it from time to time."

Trudi laughed. "Don't worry, Miss. We'd always wondered what your study looked like."

Mrs Hampshire smiled and said, "I don't think you'll need to see it anymore."

Marcus grinned. "Nor do we, Miss."

The Headmistress left the room and the friends followed Mike Stephens to the Jaguar.

"Happy ending?" he asked as they all climbed into the car.

"We think so," replied Marcus and Trudi together.

So did two very proud parents that evening when they heard the news.

All was well and truly forgiven now...

Chapter 22

"Our Railway"

It was the last day of the Christmas term. As Marcus and Trudi climbed on to the train to go to Royds Well, they knew it would be no ordinary day. For this was the day on which the school was taking over the railway line. From now on it would be known as the RWHS Royds Well to Banham line, being named after Royds Well High School.

After School assembly that morning the pupils and teachers would be walking to Royds Well Station for a ceremony involving Governors, the Headmistress, the local MP, Councillors and various other local dignitaries. Marcus and Trudi were to play their part, of course, and they had wanted everybody to be there who had helped them in any way.

They had racked their brains about this. Marcus' Mother, and Trudi's Father and Grandmother, were there.

Sid, the old railwayman who had given them the idea of how to save the line was also there.

So too were Jane Harding, the paper girl who had delivered the message from Trudi to Marcus, and Wendy Smith the receptionist, at the railway company. Philip Belstone, the unpleasant man who had been Regional Director of the railway company, was not there. The other directors had decided to remove him when they realised how unpopular the closure of the Banham line would be.

All in all, it was a grand reunion of Marcus and Trudi's friends and those who had been on their side.

The Headmistress spoke first. "I'm very proud of Trudi Barnes and Marcus Redlands," she said. "Without them, the school would never have been given the railway line. Of course, we are extremely grateful for the generosity of our Chairman of Governors, Mike Stephens…"

She went on to say that she hoped as many pupils as possible would get involved with the running of the railway, and to point out that the railway would continue to be run for the benefit of people living in Royds Well and Banham. George Scott, the local Member of Parliament, spoke next - and at great length.

He described Marcus and Trudi as fine examples of Royds Well pupils and praised them for their initiative in fighting to save the railway.

Mike Stephens, who had bought the railway line for the school, stood up next. "I'm going to let you into a secret," he began. "I'm just as much a fan of this railway line as Marcus and Trudi. I left it to them to have ideas about how the line could be saved, but I was just as keen as they were that they should succeed…"

A few other people spoke before it was Trudi's turn to say a few words. It seemed strange to her to be the centre of attention for all these people. She felt nervous. She felt suddenly angry, too as she remembered all the people who had stood in their way, as she and Marcus tried to save the railway.

The local MP had been speaking a few minutes before. What had he talked about? Their initiative in fighting to save the railway. George Scott, on the other hand, had shown no initiative. He had made it clear that he didn't think anybody could stop the closure of the railway and he certainly did not intend to lift a finger to try. Marcus and Trudi had had a lot of trouble, of course, because of the way the local newspaper had chosen to report their campaign.

Mark Richards, whom they suspected of trying to stir up friction between them and the school, was at the ceremony. All of the teachers were present, too, and a lot of the Governors - a lot of these people had apparently been 'baying for blood,' as the Headmistress had put it, only a few weeks before.

Yes, Marcus and Trudi had felt as though they had a lot of enemies when they were fighting to save the railway. It was very tempting to say something about that now, and Trudi felt a strong urge to do so, while all those 'enemies' were basking in the glory of what she and Marcus had achieved.

Of course, she knew that wasn't what was expected of her by the school, by her Father and Grandmother and by the other friendly faces there. It might be the start of the Christmas holidays, but words would certainly be said if she used this opportunity to take revenge, at home later that day and probably at school the following term. Still, she would have taken very public 'revenge' and her enemies would be all the more shocked by being caught unawares. Consequences were something Trudi could worry about later. How very tempting it was…

Then another thought struck her. By being there, these people were admitting that she and Marcus had been right - and that they had been wrong.

She and Marcus had won - so there was no need to settle old scores. Anyway, she would have hurt too many people if she had spoken out. Her Father, her

Grandmother, Mike Stephens - they would have been as shocked as those who had not helped the campaign. She didn't want to hurt them.

"I just want to thank everybody who helped us." Trudi said what everybody would expect her to say on such an occasion. "I'd like to say a particular thank you to one person here - Sid Parkes, who has been the Station Master at Banham for more than twenty years. He'll be retiring at the end of March, but he's been such a friendly face at our local station that we'll miss him so much."

That, Trudi knew, was as much as she could say about Sid in public - as much as she could say about the man who had done more than anybody else to help them save the railway. She caught his eye - he looked pleased.

"We're very grateful to Mike Stephens for buying the railway for the school," she continued, before adding with a broad smile, "and I'm grateful to my Father and Grandmother for putting up with me while I had other things on my mind."

Trudi sat down and there was a lot of clapping and cheering from pupils and teachers.

Marcus stood up. "I'd just like to echo what Trudi has said. There are lots of people whose efforts to save the railway are really appreciated. I'm grateful to Mum too, for putting up with me."

The speeches were now over, and the ceremony was almost at an end.

"As you know," said the Headmistress, "we shall be running four trains a day on this line from now on, and we've had plenty of volunteers to help staff the stations from teachers, parents and senior pupils. A few of them would like to drive the engine as well, but you'll be pleased to know we haven't accepted their offer."

There was general laughter at the Headmistress's joke. "The official party are going to ride to Banham and back on the train," continued Mrs Hampshire. "I'm afraid the rest of you will have to return to your lessons."

Marcus and Trudi assumed that this meant them as well and made as if to join the other pupils. Mike Stephens tugged them on the shoulder.

"Where are you two going?"

"Back to school."

"I don't think so," said the businessman. "This is your success. You're entitled to ride on this train if anybody is." He turned to the Headmistress. "You don't mind if the Guardians of the Railway ride with the official party, do you, Jennifer?"

"The Guardians of the Railway?" Mrs Hampshire asked. "Who are they?"

"Marcus and Trudi. They saved the line."

The two friends were ready for the Headmistress to reply solemnly - "I certainly do mind. They must go back to their lessons at once."

Instead, she smiled at them and said, "No, of course I don't mind. This is their day. I'll speak to their teachers about it later."

So, together with the Headmistress, Mike Stephens, the local MP, some of the Governors and quite a few other people they didn't know - and Sid Parkes whom they did - they stepped onto the train.

Before the train left the station, quite a few people came up to Marcus and Trudi to congratulate them on their efforts. They were most surprised when George Scott, the Member of Parliament, did so too.

"I just wanted to say that I really admire what you have both achieved," he said, shaking them by the hand. "I wish I'd helped you now - I really didn't think anybody would be able to stop the railway company. I owe you an apology."

Trudi was watching the MP closely as he was speaking. She thought that he really meant what he was saying. She felt ashamed for even having been tempted to speak out against him and others in front of the crowd a few minutes earlier.

She laughed: "It's alright. I don't think anybody thought we could stop the railway company - we certainly didn't."

"Even so," replied the MP, "I'm sorry I didn't try to help you. Please forgive me."

"Now there's an apology I didn't expect," whispered Marcus, when George Scott was out of earshot. Trudi nodded.

By the time the train had returned to Royds Well and the various passengers on board had finished congratulating, chatting to and wishing Trudi and Marcus well, it was lunchtime. They set off to walk back to the school.

"You know," said Marcus. "School is going to seem pretty dull next term after this. We've spent this term fighting to save the railway, getting into trouble with the school and our parents, and making enemies of just about everybody. All we'll be doing next term is schoolwork."

Trudi grinned: "You'll be doing that, too, will you?"

She knew what Marcus meant, though. She expected that the afternoon would seem quite dull compared to the morning. Still, after that, it would be the Christmas holidays…

He gave her a friendly punch: "Of course I'll be working," he replied.

The afternoon was not quite as dull as they expected. The teachers - aware that the holidays were only a few hours away and the pupils could not be expected to concentrate, allowed them to play games and amuse themselves instead.

Even so, Marcus and Trudi were glad when it was four o'clock and they could escape from school for the next fortnight.

They spoke to the Station Master as they got out at Banham, "It's all worked out very well, Sid."

"It certainly has. Do you two want a mug of cocoa?"

The two pupils joined him in his office, sitting quietly as he made the drink.

"I didn't think you were going to do it; you know." The Station Master broke the silence.

"I'm not sure we did anything," replied Trudi. "You suggested that we talk to Mike Stephens again, and you told us how we could run the railway so that it made money. You deserve the credit, not us."

Sid looked at her thoughtfully: "It's nice of you to say that lass, but you know I could never take the credit for this - not if I wanted to get my pension from the railway company."

He paused then added, "Anyway, think of the other people who have helped. Mike Stephens, who bought the line for your school. The railway company agreed to pay my wages until I retire at the end of March. What you did lass, and you, lad" - he nodded at Marcus - "was to sell the idea to them. I could never have done that."

It seemed unlikely that the modest railwayman would ever admit the part he had played in trying to save the railway - so Trudi stopped trying to persuade him. Before the two friends left to go home, though, Trudi gave him a hug and Marcus shook his hand.

"You will still take an interest in the railway after you have retired, won't you? We'll still see you around?"

"Sounds like an order to me, lass." Sid laughed. "Don't you worry, I'll turn up like a bad penny to make sure you and your friends are running this railway properly. You'll soon get fed up of me, I promise you. Anyway, you're not getting rid of me yet, I don't retire until the end of March."

Trudi gave Sid another hug and Marcus shook his hand again.

"What a lovely man," said Trudi as they walked home.

"Isn't he?" agreed Marcus.

They came to the point where they went in different directions. "We must meet during the school holidays." said Trudi.

They kept that promise, visiting one another's homes while they were off school. Both enjoyed a very happy Christmas, though soon enough it was time to return to school again. Even the longest of holidays never seemed to be quite long enough...

Chapter 23

One Day in April

It was a Monday morning in early April. The sun was shining brightly, and Marcus and Trudi would have considered it a brilliant day if it had not been the first day of the summer term. Sid Parkes, the station master, had retired the previous Friday, and the two friends had been to a party to celebrate. The railway was on its own now - it was up to the pupils, parents and staff of Royds Well High School to run it.

Of course, they had gained some practice over the last few months. The gates of the station had opened at ten-to eight in the morning for as long as anybody could remember.

Since January, Sid had found that a volunteer from the school, a member of staff, parent or sixth-former had been waiting outside the gate at that time to help him.

Mostly they had just watched as he took money from passengers, gave out tickets and answered questions about connecting trains out of Royds Well.

Now Sid was no longer there, and the volunteers were doing the job. All of them knew it would be a very long time before they could do it as well as the old railwayman - he seemed to be a walking encyclopaedia of the times of trains out of Royds Well. The volunteers would have to consult their timetables.

They would be busier too, than Sid had been until recently. The ending of the bus service which had left Banham about the same time as the train meant there were usually about twice as many passengers now, on both the morning and evening trains, though neither was full.

Two volunteers were to collect the fares each morning at Banham before riding on the train to Royds Well, where another volunteer would collect passengers' tickets. Marcus and Trudi had hoped that they might be able to help, but they had been told, kindly, that they were too young.

This morning the two helpers at Banham were the Head Prefect and her Deputy. It was Rosemary Wright the Head Prefect, who served the two friends.

"Alright, you two fare dodgers!" She rattled a tin of money under their noses with a grin. "We want your money!" Trudi and Marcus obediently paid their fares.

"Just think," said Marcus as he stepped into a carriage. "If we hadn't decided to do something about it, we wouldn't have been riding on the train this morning. The railway would have closed last Friday."

"So it would!" exclaimed Trudi. She had got so used to the idea of the school taking over the line that she had completely forgotten the date on which it had been due to close.

She wondered for a moment what would have happened if the railway company had not decided to close the line. All over the country steam engines were being replaced with diesels - that would have happened on the Banham line fairly soon.

It was also unlikely that she and Marcus would have spoken to one another on the train the previous autumn. She would still think of him as someone who enjoyed playing the fool rather than using his brains, he still did that, but only occasionally now.

How would he have thought of her? She had a dim memory of a phrase he had once used when he was angry - "a stuck-up Miss Goody Two-Shoes." She hoped she wasn't like that - indeed, she was fairly sure she wasn't.

Marcus, too, was having similar thoughts. Had it not been for the notice on the platform about the railway closure, Trudi would probably have stuck her nose in a French book on that journey when they were sitting opposite one another. He would have continued to think of her as some kind of snob who sucked up to adults, rather than the real human being he had discovered her to be. The loss would have been his.

How would she have thought of him? As an intelligent boy who played the fool. A fair judgement really, if he thought about it. He had though, become much more serious and hardworking over the last term, as nearly all of his teachers had commented on his last School Report. Trudi must have been a good influence on him, he supposed - his Mother certainly thought so and he wasn't going to argue with her!

"Penny for your thoughts." Trudi smiled at Marcus' earnest face.

"I was just thinking about that day last October when you told me off for kicking your heel..."

"With good reason!"

"... actually some kids from the youth club pushed me into you."

"A likely story." She grinned.

"It happens to be true... and then I had to sit opposite you because they had pinched all the other seats."

"It must have been terrible for you," she smiled.

"It was. I was just relieved to think that you would soon have your nose in a French book, and we wouldn't have to talk or sit there looking at one another."

"Is that what you were thinking?" Trudi sounded surprised. Marcus hoped he had not hurt her feelings.

"It was."

"I had a feeling that you were looking at me - even though you were trying to pretend that you weren't."

He blushed. "Was I?"

"I thought so."

It was strange looking back. It all seemed a very long time ago - of course, it was more than five months. When they got to school, having handed in their tickets to a teacher at Royds Well Station, they found that Miss Loxley was already in the classroom.

"The Headmistress would like to see you as soon as possible," she said, looking slightly anxious.

Trudi glanced at Marcus as if asking: "What trouble have you got me into now?" The two pupils stood dumbstruck in front of Miss Loxley.

"She did say as soon as possible," repeated their form-teacher. "I think you ought to go now." So, looking a little worried, the two set off for the Headmistress' study.

"We can't have done anything wrong yet," protested Trudi. "We haven't been back five minutes!"

Marcus said nothing. It was several months since they had last been summoned to Mrs Hampshire's office - why should she suddenly wish to see them now? The door of the office was slightly ajar, and Marcus knocked on it timidly.

"Is that Marcus and Trudi?" called a familiar voice.

"Do come in, please."

The friends entered nervously.

"Shut the door, please - and you may sit down." The solemn voice of the Headmistress made Marcus and Trudi anxious. Mrs Hampshire smiled: "How was your journey to school this morning?"

Marcus and Trudi were amazed. This was the last question they had expected to be asked.

"Very good, thanks Miss," replied Trudi.

"What I really meant was, how did our pupils and teachers manage this morning? I presume you travelled on the train?"

Suddenly the two friends understood why Mrs Hampshire wanted to see them. She was checking up on the railway - her railway.

Marcus grinned: "They were doing a very good job, Miss," he replied.

"Good." Mrs Hampshire looked pleased. "You will no doubt be looking forward to being able to help on the railway yourselves in a few years' time? After all…" The Headmistress continued. "… you were the Guardians of the Railway, so Mike Stephens tells me." Trudi smiled. "We are." She said.

She paused. "We've had a lot of volunteers - staff, sixth formers and parents - to help with the railway and we've drawn up a rota for it. We'll need to keep it running during the school holidays as well of course, but I'm sure we'll be able to do that."

There was silence for a moment before she added, "I want you two to keep an eye on things, I know how much you care about the railway. If there's anything wrong, please tell either me or Mr McCann.

"Mr McCann also wanted to get together a small group of people to keep an eye on the running of the railway - the number of people riding on it, the amount of fares we are collecting, that sort of thing. I said that you would expect to be members of that group."

"Thank you, Miss."

Marcus remembered the first time they had been to the Headmistress's study, after the half-term holiday the previous October. Then, she had been furious that they had used the name of the school in their campaign to save the railway, and they had been terrified of her. How things had changed!

The school's name was officially connected with the railway now - the school owned it. Whatever harsh things Mrs Hampshire had said then, she had said plenty of nice things about Marcus and Trudi since and now she wanted them to help run the railway.

"Do you think anybody else would like to join the little group?" asked the Headmistress.

Trudi hesitated: "Sid - Sid Parkes, the retired station master might be interested," she said.

"Yes, I was thinking about him," replied the Headmistress. "We would need to get permission from the railway company, as they are paying his pension, but I don't think they would refuse."

The Headmistress was silent for a moment or so. Then she said, "You know, I was very worried about whether this would make any money for the school. We've been fortunate - the railway company carried on paying Sid after Christmas, so we've only had to pay our share of the driver's wages. The railway is bringing quite a lot of money into the school - we might need some ideas about how to spend it."

Marcus grinned. "I've got a model railway set Miss, and I could do with a few carriages for that…"

Still smiling, the Headmistress replied, "… and I've got a school assembly to take - be off with the pair of you."

Marcus glanced at his watch. Almost nine o'clock, they had better dash. He started to run, and Trudi followed suit.

Mrs Hampshire walked out of her office: "Marcus and Trudi?"

"Yes, Miss." They stopped running and turned to face her.

"You may be helping to run the railway, but I'll run the school on my own, if you don't mind. You'll *walk* in the corridors," she winked, "and I'll give you time to get into assembly."

Marcus and Trudi might have thought that they had won - but Mrs Hampshire had certainly had the last word!

The End

Acknowledgements

I would like to thank Ann Cryer, MP for Keighley from 1997 to 2010 and President of the Keighley and Worth Valley Railway Preservation Society, for permission to use the wording of the plaque commemorating her husband Bob Cryer in the Dedication at the start of this book.

I originally wrote this story by hand in the summer of 1996. The Keighley and Worth Valley Railway was certainly an inspiration for it as was a public transport museum in Low Moor Bradford, Transperience, which was sadly only open for two years between 1995 and 1997.

I should also like to thank various other people who have supported and assisted with this project.

Tony Drake Curator of the Bluebell Railway replied to an e-mail and provided me with some valuable information.

I find that the paintings of Malcolm Root take me back to the steam era – exactly where I need to be when I am working on this book! The memoirs of Granville Dobson about his time as a fireman at the former locomotive shed at Low Moor Bradford were fascinating.

Alec Suchi, specialist bookseller, saw my manuscript after I had word processed it five years ago and has since encouraged me to "do something with it."

Others have read the work too before its publication as "Guardians of the Railway" and I am grateful to them for any comments they have passed.

Finally, a Big Thank You to Daisa Morgan and team at Daisa Publishing.

BV - #0033 - 090120 - C0 - 198/129/14 - PB - 9781916225114